Aldabra

Juan de Nova

LES COMORRES

La Grande
Mohilba
Johanna
Mayotte

Cap d'Ambre
Baie de Diego Suarez
Port Louquez
Nossi... Baie Vohimar

AFRIQUE

Baie de Bombétoka

Mozambique

Cap St André

CANAL DE MOZAMBIQUE

OCÉAN

15°S

Ts.iana Ka...

Baie d'Anton-Gil
Tintingue
I. Ste Marie
Foulpointe
Tamatave

Tananarivo

Andévourande

INDIEN

Ile de France
Port Louis
St Denis
Ile Bourbon

Mourondava

Amboudiharo

Matatane

Tropique

Baie St Augustin

Baie de Ste Luce

Cap Ste Marie
Port Dauphin

MADAGASCAR

445 Kilom. ou 100 Lieues

Coupe de l'île par Tananarivo

THE
MAROONS

LOUIS TIMAGÈNE HOUAT

THE
MAROONS

Translated from the French by
Aqiil Gopee with Jeffrey Diteman

Introduction by
Shenaz Patel

RESTLESS BOOKS
NEW YORK · AMHERST

Introduction copyright © 2024 Shenaz Patel
Translation copyright © 2024 Aqiil M. Gopee with Jeffrey Diteman
First published as *Les Marrons* by Ebrard, Paris, 1844

Map of Madagascar (1858) courtesy of Grafissimo.

First Restless Books paperback edition February 2024

Paperback ISBN: 9781632063557
Library of Congress Control Number: 2023945246

This work is published with the support of the National Endowment for the Arts and the New York State Council on the Arts.

Cover design by Jamie Keenan
Cover illustration by Nicolas Etienne
Set in Garibaldi by Tetragon, London

Printed in the United States

1 3 5 7 9 10 8 6 4 2

RESTLESS BOOKS
NEW YORK · AMHERST
www.restlessbooks.org

CONTENTS

UNSILENCING A (HI)STORY

This is the story of an overlooked book.

Louis Timagène Houat's *Les Marrons* can be deemed a tour de force—a work of great literary quality, as well as an exceptional testimony of nineteenth-century slavery in the Indian Ocean, revealing the struggle carried out within the colonies themselves, a struggle which would ultimately result in the abolition of slavery by the great colonizing powers.

And yet, this novel, published in 1844 in Paris, remained "absent" and unknown to the public for a century and a half until its rediscovery by Raoul Lucas, the Réunionese researcher who would shed light on its pages for a contemporary audience.

And this tells us a lot about the silencing power of those who write official history.

Les Marrons is probably the very first Réunionese novel. It was published at a time when Réunion Island, then known as Bourbon Island, and its neighbor, Île de France, now called Mauritius, played a key role in the West's enrichment. Indeed, during the eighteenth century, these two islands situated in the middle of the Indian Ocean served as crucial waypoints for Dutch, Portuguese, Spanish, French, and English ships— a vital stopover on the grand route to India, where they would acquire spices, silks, and various other goods.

Initially serving as mere resupply stops, the twin islands swiftly garnered recognition as promising destinations for settlement, offering opportunities for the cultivation of cotton, sugar, coffee, cocoa, and indigo. This, however, required a labor force. Thus, starting in the seventeenth century, a substantial slave trade was organized.

When speaking of the slave trade, which led, through the centuries, to the displacement of tens of millions of Africans reduced to a state of slavery, we tend to focus mainly on the transatlantic trade. For years, the focus of historians has been on the fate of the eleven to thirteen million people deported from Africa to the Americas between the eighteenth and nineteenth centuries. By comparison, the Indian Ocean trade has been largely overlooked. In the span of two centuries, roughly four to five million African natives were captured and subsequently enslaved on the islands of the Indian Ocean—though this figure is likely underestimated, given that the region's ship- and land-owners tended to under-declare their slaves to escape higher taxation and to avoid getting caught when, following the official abolition of the trade at the start of the nineteenth century, they continued illegally bringing African captives as slaves to the islands.

This is the story of an exiled book.

Exiled, like its writer.

Considered the first novel to come out of Réunion Island, *Les Marrons* was published in Paris, where its author, Réunionese writer Louis Timagène Houat, had been deported.

Houat's destiny is an exceptional one—the kind nourished by those islands where history stirs life into a unique, fertile, volcanic disarray.

According to various documents, his surname originated from Ouattara, his father's name. His father, a member of Guinea's Bambara tribe, arrived in Île de France toward the end of the eighteenth century before eventually settling in Bourbon in 1806. It was on August 12, 1809, in Bourbon, that Louis Timagène was born. To contemporary observers, he is a mystery lying in plain sight: how could someone like young Louis Timagène, in this distant colony where those considered Black were not allowed to attend school until 1845, exhibit such remarkable brilliance from such an early age—to the point of wanting, at sixteen, to build a small school of his own by the river in the island's capital city, Saint-Denis? Could family connections account for such precocity?

Indeed, Houat was the nephew of Lislet Geoffroy, himself an enigma to the intelligentsia of his time. Born on Bourbon Island in 1755, to Niama, a Senegalese princess enslaved at the age of nine, and Jean-Baptiste Geoffroy, a French engineer, Lislet never went to school and yet became one of the greatest scientists of his generation. An illustrious astronomer, botanist, meteorologist, cartographer, and geologist, he was the first Black man to be elected a corresponding member of Paris's Académie des Sciences, in 1786, under the direct patronage of the Duke de La Rochefoucauld-Liancourt, a cousin of King Louis XVI. In the fight for the abolition of slavery and human rights, he was held up as a symbol in the progressive intellectual circles of the time, on the eve of the French Revolution.

Was Louis Timagène Houat inspired by this illustrious uncle?

In any case, he was quickly singled out by Bourbon's settlers as a dangerous anti-slavery advocate—someone who needed to be promptly dealt with if the status quo was to be preserved. He was a man with a brilliant mind, who helped promote the circulation in Bourbon of the *Revue des Colonies*, a monthly paper printed in Paris by Cyrille Bissette, an abolitionist from Martinique who also founded the Société des Amis des Noirs.

On December 13, 1835, Houat, then twenty-six, was arrested. Allegedly involved in what would later be dubbed the "Saint-André conspiracy," he was accused of having incited a revolt against the settlers, aiming to abolish slavery on the island of Bourbon and establish an "African Republic." He spent eight months in jail awaiting his trial, an imprisonment he described in his *Lettre d'un prévenu dans l'affaire de l'île Bourbon* (Letter from a defendant in the Bourbon Island case), published by the *Revue des Colonies* in September 1836. The *Revue* also assiduously followed Houat's momentous trial, which unfolded from December 1836 to June 1837, ending with him and four others sentenced to life behind bars.

Due to blatant violations of due process—a result of the governor's grip on Bourbon's judicial system—and thanks to an amnesty granted by King Louis-Philippe I in 1837, Houat's sentence was eventually commuted to political exile: he would have to endure a seven-year banishment from the colony.

He thus found himself in Paris, where he sought the company of other abolitionists. In 1838, Houat published his first "literary" work: *Un proscrit de l'île Bourbon à Paris* (An exile from Bourbon Island in Paris), in which he offered a poetic account of his imprisonment and subsequent banishment from the colony. And then, four years before the abolition of slavery was made official in France in 1848, under the patronage of the Ebrard bookstore located on the Passage des Panoramas, Houat published his first and apparently only novel: *Les Marrons*.

This is the story of suppressed books.

Les Marrons tells the story of Frême, an escaped slave living in the island's remote mountains with Marie, a White woman. In this regard, Houat can practically be deemed a trailblazer.

In 1781, under the pseudonym "Joachim Schwartz," Nicolas de Condorcet published *Réflexions sur l'esclavage des nègres* (*Thoughts on the Enslavement of Negroes*), an essay denouncing slavery as a crime. In 1815, Abbé Henri Grégoire, a fellow member of the Société des Amis des Noirs, published *De la traite et de l'esclavage des noirs* (*On the Trade and Enslavement of Blacks*), a powerful anti-slavery polemic. However, literary writers seemed to struggle in tackling the subject.

Toward the close of the twentieth century, in 1994, on the French TV show *La Marche de l'Histoire* (The March of History), writer and critic Gérard Gengembre raised the question of why literature seemed to have failed to address the fundamental issue of slavery, despite the remarkable proliferation of texts inspired by the French Revolution. "One cannot help but be struck by the observation that while the condition of Black people in general and the specific issue of slavery are not entirely overlooked in Romantic literature, they remain relatively minor topics of discussion," he said. "This may be one of the most significant contradictions within Revolutionary-era literature, as it failed to fully embrace its own revolutionary message. Perhaps this can be attributed to the Revolution itself falling short of realizing its guiding principles in their entirety."

Despite the revolutionary assertion of *Liberté, Egalité, Fraternité* (Freedom, Equality, Fraternity) at the core of its 1789 Declaration of the Rights of Man and of the Citizen, France hesitated to take a definitive stance on the matter of slavery. Despite the official abolition of the slave trade in 1794, Napoleon reinstated its legality in the colonies in 1802.

Eighteenth- and nineteenth-century literature reveals how arduous its authors found the task of writing about slavery. Bernardin de Saint-Pierre was one of the first writers to broach the subject in his novel *Paul et Virginie (Paul & Virginia)* in 1788, although contemporary readers may object that he did so from the point of view of the "good master." Alexandre Dumas, celebrated for his *Les Trois Mousquetaires (The Three Musketeers)* and *Le Comte de Monte-Cristo (The Count of Monte Cristo)*, wrote a denunciation of slavery in his novel *Georges*, which focused on the fight led by a Black man against White racism toward mixed-race freemen in his native Île de France at the beginning of the nineteenth century. We may also mention *Bug-Jargal*, Victor Hugo's first novel, published in 1826, which portrays the inhumane conditions imposed on Saint-Domingue's slave population prior to the 1791 uprising that led to the creation of the first independent Black republic of Haiti in 1804. As Gengembre put it, "While we may find a number of works dealing with the topic of slavery, we also find that literary history, and its capacity for the institutionalization of our collective memory, has either neglected to acknowledge them or relegated them to relatively obscure realms."

This same "obscurity" also proves relevant in the case of the United States. In *Twelve Years a Slave*, Solomon Northup offers a firsthand testimony of his experience as a Black man born free in New York, but subsequently kidnapped and enslaved for twelve years in Louisiana, nearly a decade before the American Civil War. Despite being published in 1853 and extensively cited in the abolitionist debate, this autobiography was "forgotten" for nearly a century. It was rediscovered in the early 1960s by two Louisiana historians, leading to a reprint in 1968. Eventually, it gained further recognition with a cinematic adaptation by Steve McQueen, which won the Academy Award for Best Picture in 2014.

A similar fate befell another novel, one that likely inspired Hugo in writing *Bug-Jargal*. The work in question, *Adonis ou le bon nègre, anecdote coloniale* (*Adonis; or, the Good Negro*) by Jean-Baptiste Piquenard, was first published in 1798. However, after 1836, it vanished from public attention for over a century and a half, until two successive reprints in 2005 and 2006.

This is also what happened to Louis Timagène Houat's *Les Marrons*.

This is the story of a silenced book.

In 1844, Houat published his novel *Les Marrons*, "accompanied by 14 pretty drawings" by Félix, who is speculated to have been a Parisian wood-engraver.

It would seem, however, that the book quickly faded from the collective memory. Its literary quality was certain—what, then, could be the cause of such a disappearance?

Official records show that in September 1844, Martinique's local authorities seized shipments of books declared "a threat to the public order" from two incoming ships. Over 150 copies of *Les Marrons* were among the confiscated books, alongside a critical essay by Bissette concerning a new law soon to be imposed on the slave population. After persistent complaints from the two men, the Minister of the Colonies finally stated that the books could not be sent off to any other French colony. It would take Houat and Bissette two years to retrieve their respective books, which they now understood to be subject to an implicit distribution ban.

But books have a life of their own, surpassing the will of men.

In his four-volume series called *The Cemetery of Forgotten Books*, Spanish author Carlos Ruiz Zafón posits that we do not really choose books: rather, we are chosen, adopted, by them.

This may be what Réunionese sociologist and academic Raoul Lucas felt after serendipitously rediscovering *Les Marrons* while conducting archival research at the Bibliothèque Nationale de France in Paris, at the end of the 1970s.

One can only imagine the shock, the bewilderment, the stupefaction of "discovering" a forgotten book. And the thrill of bringing it back into the world.

In 1986, a copy of the novel's first edition was found in the bequest made by the Barquisseau family to the media library of Saint-Pierre, Réunion. Raoul Lucas, in collaboration with the Centre de recherche indianocéanique (CRI), worked toward the book's reissue. In 1988, *Les Marrons* finally made its public comeback. "Nothing in our preceding readings or in our ongoing research on the question of slavery, or, more generally, of the French colonization in Bourbon and Île de France, had prepared us for what came as a shock, a revelation, and a mystery. It took us many years along with other fortunate circumstances to collect everything we now know about the author and his work," Lucas wrote in his preface to a subsequent reprint by the Association d'Insertion pour le Développement Économique et Social (AIPDES). Such is the way of silenced books.

While, in English, the verb "to silence" has been in usage for a long time, in French, it was only recently, in 2022, that it made its official appearance in the dictionary *Le Robert*.

The practice of silencing writers and their books, however, has a longstanding precedent, especially when it comes to writing official history.

Silencing the story, in other words, has always been a means of silencing history.

In his book *Silencing the Past: Power and the Production of History*, the Haitian anthropologist Michel-Rolph Trouillot delivers a powerful analysis of the fabrication of official history. What matters, he says, is not determining what history is, but how history works. History, he further argues, primarily reveals itself through the production of specific narratives, themselves shaped by important power inequalities. The powers in place not only determine what will be recorded and what will be disregarded, but also decide what will endure through memory and what will gradually or abruptly disappear. In light of this, the notion that historical narratives inherently possess a stronger claim to "truth" than literary narratives becomes increasingly dubious. The key lies in analyzing the processes and conditions through which such narratives were produced, and the ways in which the powers-that-be facilitated certain narratives while silencing others.

It is therefore important, according to Trouillot, not to underestimate the collective impact that various modes of historical production possess in shaping our understanding. And there, precisely, lies the relevance of so many works of fiction: Trouillot finds that, from the second half of the 1950s to the end of the 1960s, Americans learned more about their own history through cinema and television than through scholarly books.

This is a story that remains unclassified.

On February 9, 2018, in response to a Freedom of Information Act request submitted in January, the British Treasury published the following tweet: "Here's today's surprising #FridayFact. Millions of you have helped end the slave trade through your taxes. Did you know? In 1833, Britain used £20 million, 40% of its national budget, to buy freedom for all slaves in the Empire. The amount of money borrowed for the Slavery Abolition Act was so large that it wasn't paid off until 2015. Which means that living British citizens helped pay to end the slave trade."

While it generated many objections and corrections, this tweet nevertheless remains fundamentally accurate, as demonstrated by Kris Manjapra, associate professor of history at Tufts University, in an article published in the *Guardian* on March 29, 2018, under the title: "When will Britain face up to its crimes against humanity?"

Manjapra begins by reminding his readers that, following the 1833 Slavery Abolition Act, Great Britain indeed paid substantial compensation sums—not to the freed slaves, but to their former owners—to indemnify the latter for their "loss." To finance such an operation, the Chancellor of the Exchequer had signed an agreement with two of Europe's most famous bankers, Nathan Mayer Rothschild and his brother-in law, Moses Montefiore, whereby they would lend the British government £15 million—to which the government later added £5 million more. All in all, the compensation package represented forty percent of the government's yearly budget at the time (which would amount to some £300 billion today). The profit acquired from this compensation was passed down from one generation of the British elite to the next. "Among the descendants of the recipients of slave-owner compensation is the former Prime Minister David Cameron," Manjapra writes.

Far from being an aberration, this tweet, according to Manjapra, is "emblematic of the way legacies of slavery continue to shape life for the descendants of the formerly enslaved," as well as for British people of all backgrounds. "The legacies of slavery in Britain are not far off; they are in front of our eyes every single day," Manjapra writes. According to him, the crucial role played by Great Britain in over 500 years of trade and enslavement is often glossed over by highlighting the nation's role in the process of abolition. In this regard, it is interesting to note that the British abolitionists, arguing that slavery was contrary to God's will, had resolved to encourage their fellow citizens to face slaves, look them in the eye, and recognize them as fellow human beings. To do so, they widely distributed the autobiographies of formerly enslaved individuals, such as Ignatius Sancho, Olaudah Equiano, and Mary Prince. Their aim was to present the British public with firsthand accounts of enslaved Black individuals, hoping that hearing their voices through their own writings would evoke empathy for their suffering and galvanize opposition against their oppression. That would potentially enable the British public to "look into the eyes of the enslaved and to see a person staring back."

It might have been precisely this potential that led to books such as *Les Marrons* being doomed to obscurity.

This is the story of a book that remembers.

Houat wrote his book with the explicit will to shed light, for the French public, on the horrific conditions that slaves were forced to endure under the French Empire, and on the treatment reserved for maroons under the Code Noir.

But to do so, he didn't write a pamphlet. He wrote a novel.

He wrote through the prism of imagination, employing the tools of literary and linguistic creation.

The words we use matter. They shape our reality.

In 1838, Frederick Douglass fled from his master's property in Baltimore and found refuge in Massachusetts. Seven years later, he published *Narrative of the Life of Frederick Douglass, an American Slave*, wherein he spoke in great detail of his experience of enslavement. The success of the book unfortunately brought him a level of recognition that jeopardized his safety. Encouraged by his abolitionist friends, he left the United States for England, to avoid being captured and sent back into slavery under the Fugitive Slave Act. For eight years, and until he was re-bought by English philanthropists and officially declared a freeman on December 12, 1846, Douglass was considered a "fugitive slave." Had his story unfolded in Réunion Island, he would have been called a maroon.

Topography also determines the conditions for freedom. In Réunion Island, the steep and precipitous terrain stands as a visible testament to the territory's volcanic origins, providing us with a glimpse into the hardships that molded the lives of the fugitives. While in the United States, a number of slaves managed to flee the South and find refuge in the anti-slavery states of the North, the limited expanse of Réunion Island, consisting of only 2,500 square kilometers, left little room for escape. Therefore, escaping slaves had no choice but to take to Réunion's heights, characterized by steep mountains and inaccessible calderas. There, they created what would later come to be known as the "Kingdom of the Heights," or "Kingdom of the Interior" (as opposed to the coastal areas, occupied by the colonizers). In these untamed spaces, the wild offered its protection solely to the most daring, for the wilderness was rough.

According to some etymological sources, the term "maroon" comes from the Spanish *cimarrón*, derived from *cima* (summit), and meaning "summit dweller." Alternatively, the word may have originated in Haiti, and more precisely from its first inhabitants, the Arawak Indians, who called the island Ayiti (meaning "the land of high mountains"). The Arawaks used the term *símara* to talk about animals, most frequently pigs, gone back to a feral state after having been domesticated. According to this theory, following Christopher Columbus's 1492 colonization of the island, which he dubbed Hispaniola, the word *cimarrón* emerged around 1540 to refer to fugitive Indigenous people who resisted enslavement.

The tales of maroons vividly illustrate that throughout the Atlantic and Indian Oceans, men and women consistently defied the shackles of their enslavement. Such stories show that they have always, whether alone or collectively, fiercely fought to escape it. In some cases, they even refused, from the outset, to submit to the will of a master. Lislet Geoffroy, Louis Timagène Houat's uncle, recounts that, during an expedition with the botanist Commerson to the island's volcano in 1771, they came across a Black woman from Madagascar named Simanandé, and her son Tsifaron. Simanandé had taken refuge on one of the mountain's peaks after successfully escaping upon her arrival on the island, before she could be taken to her future master's property. The cold had caught her by surprise, and she had sought sanctuary in one of the mountain's caves.

When sent to hunt down fugitives, maroon hunters did not always succeed in returning with their intended targets. If the slaves were killed in the chase, carrying their bodies over the uneven terrain would be too cumbersome. As a result, the hunters would often bring back only a severed ear, which they would then affix to a board displayed in the public square of their village to announce the capture.

Centuries later, bringing back a book about maroons holds a different significance—it symbolizes the retrieval of a voice rather than a mere body part. It amounts to *re-membering* history's dislocated body.

This is the story of a pioneering book.

And that is why Aqiil Gopee and Jeffrey Diteman's brilliant translation of *The Maroons* is essential.

It brings to the English-speaking world a previously unheard and yet crucial voice of the abolitionist fight.

In *The Maroons*, Houat shows that being a maroon entails more than simply escaping the confines of a plantation and employing extraordinary survival strategies. By establishing settlements in the elevated regions of the island, the maroons aspire to forge a new world—a world of freedom that upholds and empowers the inherent dignity of every human being.

In post-abolition colonial literature, the character of the maroon was largely used to embody malevolent forces. For example, in Réunion Island lore, Kala, a maroon woman, became a witch figure invoked to frighten children into obedience. Contemporary literature, however, has reclaimed the figure of the maroon, making it an anti-colonial metaphor for freedom.

Rediscovering *The Maroons* today participates in our awareness of the creolization of the world.

Houat not only presents the dream of an open society, where the fusion of races leads to peace and harmony, but also highlights the significance of racial blending occurring in Bourbon as a precursor to a global movement. Embracing this novel takes the reader on a transformative journey that transcends simplistic notions of race-mixing.

Édouard Glissant said that for creolization to occur, the cultural elements brought together should be "equal in value," and not merely persisting in a relationship of dominance.

Houat actively participates in this transformative process by centering his book on the maroons—their voices, their struggles, and their vibrant lives pulsating like a desperate heartbeat. In doing so, he restores them to our collective and individual consciousness in their fundamental essence as human beings. "Isn't the act of forgetting through alienation, ignorance, or arrogance indicative of underlying serious unresolved issues?" This question, as formulated by Glissant in 2008, in *Tous les jours de mai: Manifeste pour l'abolition de tous les esclavages* (Every day of May: Manifesto for the abolition of all slavery), continues to ring true today. "As long as we will listen privately and individually to the world's woes and joys, or that we will privately and individually express our own woes and joys, we will necessarily be shortening our own memories and will encourage the mis-knowing of that of others," Glissant writes. He calls for "a conjoining of memories, a converging of generosities, knowledge that is fundamentally impetuous, and which we all need, individuals and communities alike, wherever we may stand. To pool memories, to use some memories to liberate others, is to open all paths to Global Relation."

This translation of *The Maroons* contributes to this project. To remember our individual and collective memories, and in so doing, inscribe them lastingly into the mesh of a richer world—richer because it is less forgetful, less ignorant.

After *Les Marrons*, Louis Timagène Houat eventually settled in France, became a doctor at the King's court, and published books on homeopathic medicine, of which he was an early proponent. Judicially exiled from his island for seven years, he was sociologically banished from the collective memory for over a century and a half. But the rediscovery of his extraordinary novel has made it possible to rescue him from that silence.

The vaults of history are full of voices still to be unearthed.

SHENAZ PATEL

Translated from the French by Lisa Ducasse

FOREWORD

Le Morne Brabant, a 1,824-foot volcanic mountain, looms over the southwestern tip of Mauritius, my home island. Cradled by a pristine lagoon—so clear that you can see the belt of pale reefs poking like vertebrae through the surface—it is lush, nurturing an intricate ecosystem of endemic fauna and flora that thrives upon its slopes and inside its hidden caves. At the foot of the mountain, at the heart of the wooded recess now grimly known as the Valley of the Bones, a stone stela has been erected: the Slave Route Monument. It is said that the Africans—most of whom were abducted from Madagascar and Mozambique—enslaved by the French would climb all the way up its treacherous peak to escape the horrors of the plantations.* It is also said that, when faced with the choice between plummeting to their deaths and yielding to the patrols of White men sent to retrieve them, they favored the former, taking

---

* I resist the term "slave," in acknowledgment of the fact that slavery was not a state of being, but a thing imposed.

the plunge into either the ocean or the jagged grounds below.

This book is about such people, called maroons—"dwellers of the peaks"—trapped in the devastating beauty of such landscapes. The protagonists of Louis Timagène Houat's *Les Marrons* (1844), Réunion Island's very first novel, are left with no choice but to tame the wilderness as they are hunted by their White enslavers. As Shenaz Patel reminds us in her introduction, the "topography" of places "builds the conditions of freedom," and it is across the island's riotous savannahs, within its deep ravines and upon its vertiginous mountains that the characters find solace and community as they await liberation from an improbable sovereign beyond the seas.

The story in this book might come from an island, but it is not insular. Its translation for the first time into English aims at dismantling the hegemony that North America seems to have established over the historiography of slavery. The transatlantic trade route was but one of the many itineraries of human trafficking that involved the African continent, and it is imperative that we break the historic silence surrounding trans-Saharan, Indian Ocean, and Mascarene (including the islands of Mauritius, Réunion, and Rodrigues) economies of enslavement. This goes beyond contextual comparison, as those networks were intimately connected, their histories shared, and based upon the shattering, capture, and estrangement of the same families, the same tribes, the same peoples.

The Mascarene islands, in particular, represent a microcosm of this abomination. Some of Houat's contemporaries such as Théodore Pavie and Leconte de Lisle have also spun tales of maroonage that offer portholes into the dynamics of enslavement within the confines of an island, revealing, in a literary miniature, the structures and discourses that were unfurling elsewhere in the world to dehumanize and justify the subjugation of Black Africans. However, Houat's voice cuts against the grain of that literature, and enlightens it, by endowing, for the first time, a semblance of voice and agency to the French empire's most oppressed subalterns. While rooted in good intentions and a staunchly abolitionist stance, Théodore Pavie's *Une chasse aux nègres marrons* (A hunt for brown Negroes, 1845) or Leconte de Lisle's *Sacatove* (1846), for instance, present enslaved and marooned characters who remain captive to the White gaze, encased in the mold of the noble savage, at best. Evidence for their humanity is discussed with the ordinary violence of abstraction: absent from every conversation about their fate, the maroons lurk as unseen and inarticulate creatures of legend who haunt the woods:

"On your island, Providence has put neither reptiles nor ferocious beasts," replied the doctor, "it was reserved for the Europeans to give birth to a variety of the human species that I would gladly call the man of the woods."

As this concluding line from *Une chasse aux nègres marrons* suggests, the scientization of race, which was gaining traction in Europe at the time, often surfaces in conversations between the characters. The Creole character in Théodore Pavie's tale, named so because of his creolized, "bastardized" identity as a French settler born in the colony, is obsessed with his race, and rehashes it to get over his insecurity of being in the presence of Frenchmen from the mainland: "But we are White, as White as the biggest plantation owners, and the spade is the tool of the Blacks: that is a known fact." Leconte de Lisle's Sacatove, who requests death at the hands of his vengeful enslaver, holds on to a dark ray of hope as he utters his last words: "Do it again, master. Sacatove is unhappy now, he does not like the woods anymore, and would like to go to the great country of the good Lord, where the Whites and the Blacks live like brothers!" Frême, the hero of Louis Timagène Houat's masterpiece, offers a more sober reflection:

> They use the same money they gain from slavery to promote and maintain it. And beyond money, they still promote the ideas of color, race, domination, ships. Everything they get

from our labor is proof that slavery works: sugar, coffee, cocoa, cotton, pepper, cloves, nutmeg. Go figure! Besides, how far away is Europe? A deep, wide sea separates us from them, and they have all kinds of things besides us to think about. They don't see us, don't know us; they might be thinking all kinds of things about us. I think they'll take care of those close to them and will forget us because we are far away. They'll take care of the woods and the animals. Not us. They'll make laws, like they do here, for the preservation of plants, fisheries, horses, dogs, and birds; but not for our preservation, nothing to improve our lot. Nobody will care about our freedom . . .

Incipient fantasies of race and color were indeed realized as they got codified into law. Corresponding legal instruments, from the Code Noir enacted by Louis XIV in 1685 to the kangaroo courts established in the colonies to punish and execute maroons, remind us of the arbitrariness of legislation, and of its suspect sense of morality, particularly when it is written by, and in favor of, those who invent their privileges. Standing at the front line of colonial law enforcement were, of course, the police forces, or rather, a prototype thereof: as one of Houat's characters puts it, "the wicked little Whites that they hire to hunt you down like dogs, and to whom they pay so many francs."

Louis Timagène Houat, accused of sedition for his abolitionist stance, wrote this chilling letter in prison:

Saint-Denis (Bourbon Island), May 4, 1836*

Dear Editor,

I have been unjustly locked up for almost five months now, under the most senseless accusation. A friend of mine has just informed me here in this jail that he is leaving for France at once; I seize this fortunate occasion to address these few words to you, although the imminence of this brave young man's departure only allows me to write to you very briefly. I will write to you in detail some other time, if the wickedness of others does not prevent me from doing so.

Although Bourbon Island has so far been designated as the French colony least tainted by prejudices, your country's clergy has not been impressed by the praises that biased, privileged people have sung in its honor.

It was easy for you to recognize, in the little that I had the chance to write to you (if you received it, for here they have no qualms about intercepting and unsealing letters

* Translated from "Lettre d'un prévenu dans l'affaire de l'île Bourbon," *Revue des Colonies*, 3ᵉ année, no. 3, septembre 1836, pp. 117–122.

deemed suspicious), where things still stand in Bourbon, whatever one may say. You are not unaware that the same interests, as well as the same passions, are present here as in the French Antilles. You are not unaware of how easy it is in our colonies to get rid of one or more mulattoes or slaves. One has only to accuse them of a plot to kill the Whites, and the deed is done.

In 1810, a colonist, a real schemer, wishing to show himself off to the English government, in whose service he was working, and acquire a higher employment, fabricated in his own way a conspiracy supposedly formed by colored men. As a result of this fine invention, J.-M. Perier and several others were imprisoned; but soon the English government, discovering the scheme, had them released and gave them justice. The freed man who is one of my accusers has just come out of the workshop of this colonist and still has a wife and children who are slaves!

Well, today I and twenty-five other slaves and free people, most of whom I had neither seen nor known, were informed that we had plotted against the lives and property of the Whites; but the accusations against us went too far, and the atrocious slanders of which they are composed are already being recognized as absurd and implausible.

On the simple allegation of a slave, a passive instrument of a vile privileged person, to whom it has surely been said: You will be paid and you will be set free if you go through with the accusation, or on the words of a freedman, shameless, greedy, certainly bribed, citizens and fathers of irreproachable families were torn from their huts and thrown into jail in December 1835. When will this end? When will the colonies no longer be the scene of such tragedies?

Rumor had it that I held the works of metropolitan philanthropists in high esteem; that I liked to welcome the weak and the unfortunate; that I was pitted against the privileged; and that I maintained a correspondence with several abolitionists, and notably with you. That was all it took for me to be stigmatized as one of the vilest enemies of the colony, and from that moment on, there was a price on my head.

You have learned about Paul's ordeal, who was in charge of placing a few copies of the *Revue des Colonies* (I wrote to you about it). You have also understood the harassment he had to endure, as well as one of your correspondents who has since stopped keeping you informed of news from Bourbon. I thought it was my duty to put myself in the place of this friend, with your approval, of course. I was not afraid, whatever the cost, to work for a just and legitimate cause, and I said that I would receive the *Revue des Colonies*, that I would always subscribe to it, because no court in the world would be able to reasonably forbid it. I claimed that I desired emancipation, that if France ordered emancipation, and if in the colony a kind of league, such as that called the *Association*, came to resist the mother country by arms, I would remain forever on the side of the established government, and that I would not desert the side of the oppressed. Oh! I am already part of a conspiracy! Houat is a mulatto who must be killed or deported, or, much better, left to rot in prison!

In the meantime, news arrived from France concerning the incidental discussion that had taken place in the Chamber of Deputies on the subject of the additional credit for the colonies. Immediately afterwards, several colonists, urged on by their delegates, wrote insulting protests in the districts against the honorable Isambert, and solicited only men of color to sign them, telling them that refusal on their part would be proof that they were negrophiles and that they wanted to see in Bourbon the bloody triumph of a revolt by the Blacks. I loudly denounced such an iniquity and, as a matter of course, none of us wanted to have our names associated with it. The protests were quashed. However, Mr. Vinson, a doctor, mayor, colonial councilor, and editor of the *Indicateur Colonial*, seeing their project foiled, felt the need to conceal the defeat, to publish through the newspaper he edits that, "Many men of color have hastened to write and sign a formal denial to H. Isambert."

I cannot bear such impudence, and in order to respond to this utterly deceptive claim, I sent him a letter on behalf of the whole population he has just slandered, with a request to have it inserted in the next issue of his newspaper; but my answer, although decent and reserved, was dismissed by the colonial councilors and remains unpublished. It was accused of *negrophilia*, as was its author . . . Oh! Enough of this! Some wretches were bribed to accuse me and soon I was publicly designated as one of the leaders of a conspiracy hatched by God knows who.

However, I was not at all frightened by claptrap of this kind that was circulating on the island; my conscience made me strong, and I went about my usual life, when one morning, December 15, 1835, I heard a knock at my door! It was Mr. Collet, a police inspector, who came to roust me from bed, telling me that he had to search my house and that he was the bearer of a warrant against me! In short, he took my papers, he triumphantly came across a few issues of the *Revue des Colonies* as if it were the body of the crime, and finally, he took me to prison.

I was soon questioned by Mr. Filhol, the investigating judge. Good God! Who were my accomplices? Who were my accusers? I have as accomplices (because it is necessary to have some in this case) young people who are hardly twenty years old, most of whom I had never even seen and did not know! As for my accusers, they are firstly two slaves who belong to the same privileged house, the house of De Tourris, one of whom is a *notorious thief*, and the other of whom had sought to learn some principles of music from me; and secondly a freedman who is greedier and more dependent than the first two, and who, driven by some mysterious conspiracy, had been introduced to me by a privileged man, and who, in order to trick me, had come to implore my friendship!

But now these vile accusers have given us an idea of what happened at the Tower of Babel: confusion is in their words, lies abound, and if there is any justice in Bourbon, their slanderous absurdities can only fall back on themselves and on those who supported them.

Be that as it may, and although they found at my place, as at the places of the other defendants, neither papers nor weapons, in short, nothing that could justify the accusation of conspiracy, I was placed under a detention order and I am imprisoned until further notice under the specious and absurd pretext of *conspiracy with the aim of stirring up civil war by leading the slaves to take up arms against citizens!*

Also these gentlemen of the police have since believed that, to support, at the very least, the atrocious depositions of the accusers, they had to force a man from the White population (whom they nevertheless found it necessary to imprison, and who admitted having been paid for it) to address an anonymous letter to me in the jail of Saint-Denis. This letter, full of the most deceitful as well as the most honorable words, was supposed (and would have passed as such, were it not for its inevitable inconsistencies) to have been addressed to me by unknown accomplices. They had planned to have it handed over to me while I was in the presence of the guard, just so that the latter could lay his hands on it and prove my guilt! But God be praised! Young Victor Harel, who was charged with this unique task and whom the police had tricked with the promise that he would not be prosecuted for a forgery of which he was accused, felt his heart fail him, and did not have enough villainy in his soul to accomplish the deed. He returned the letter to the police inspector who had given it to him, claiming that he had not been allowed to see me! See and decide for yourself, my fellow citizen and brother!

On the seventh of April, during the trial of his forgery case, Harel could not help but publicly declare that he was quite surprised to be facing justice, given that the police had told him he would not be prosecuted if he would denounce me as per their instructions. He claimed that he was hence seizing this opportunity to make it known, from now on, that all the accusations made by him against several people were false, and that they had been inspired by the police.

Thanks to the remorse that took hold of young Harel, his conscience could not bear all that he had been tasked with. The day after his conviction and in front of all the prisoners he spewed out all the charges that he had been charged to lay against us by the police, and every day he made new revelations in this regard. In short, he intends to reveal in court, during the examination of our case, the wickedness of those who had pushed him to trick us. In due course I will give you proper notice of things.

Among the hateful people who want our destruction, Messrs. Testart and Vinson, colonial councilors, were annoyed not to be able to serve on the front line. The first, along with several others, has apparently asked the governor to try us in the district court.

The other had the cowardice to call us criminals, as we languish in chains, and in the most ignominious way, writing about us in his privileged newspaper (*l'Indicateur Colonial*) in an attempt to degrade us and to consign us to public execration by sullying our names and amplifying the slanderous accusations brought against us.

I repeat, we have been detained for nearly five months, and the indictment chamber has not yet issued a ruling. Most of the colored population has already been interrogated. They have been handed over to informants of all kinds and have seen themselves prey to the most unjust suspicions as a result of the atrocious activities of the police. It is also said that there are at least 1,800 pages of writing for the inquiry alone, and 700 for the report of the investigating judge. However, we are made to hope that, for those of our people who will be indicted, the trials will open over the course of the next month.

As for me, I am resigned to whatever might befall me, as I have already told them. Let the privileged defend me, or judge me, or condemn me, and although I know I will not appear before my peers, I will present myself, unafraid, in court. It will undoubtedly be necessary for me to go through whatever our miserable oppressors have devised, until it pleases God to change things for the better. It is now up to you to stigmatize such persecution, to avenge the innocent people cruelly condemned by the colonial courts!

L. T. HOUAT

Houat's voice, both in this letter and in his novella, retains its urgency. It compels us to consider the prehistory of racist structures that prevail, to shake their foundations. In the wake of the conversations generated by the Black Lives Matter movement and the calls to abolish the police, owing to the bursts of violence they keep perpetrating—as they always have—against Black people, it is more important than ever to research, understand, and unbuild the monstrous legacies that colonialism and enslavement have bequeathed to us.

A practical step forward, as embodied in this book, would be to listen to the stories that survive, to recover them from silencing.

AQIIL GOPEE

A NOTE ON THE TRANSLATION

Considering that this is a first translation of a work of great historical interest, we felt it important to maintain meticulous fidelity to Louis Timagène Houat's message. On the spectrum from literal to free approaches to translation, this text lies toward the literal end, at least in terms of content. While we have taken substantial liberties with the syntax and sentence structure of the original, we have sought to preserve every detail of the story. This results in a translation that presents the author's message in its entirety, conveyed in a style that is meant to serve as a workable equivalent, rather than a mimicry, of the original voice. Overly literal translations from the French tend to alienate English-speaking readers through heavy abstraction, a preponderance of nouns over verbs, and sentences that drag on so long as to become unwieldy. Overly free translations run the risk of subsuming the author's voice entirely into that of the translator's, failing to do justice to the writer's idiosyncrasies.

On a stylistic level, we were led by a desire to produce a translation that would be both faithful to the tone of the original and comprehensible to contemporary readers. In general, the aim was to evoke the feel of a nineteenth-century narrative without being overly quaint, archaic, or grandiose. We have sought to avoid anachronism by eschewing any terms that were coined after the 1840s, but we recognize that the idea of translating a book in the manner that it would have been translated at the time is illusory. All in all, far from leading to a flattening of its style, I find that the contradictory constraints of translating in an old-fashioned manner for a contemporary audience have led to a vibrant, unique voice for this work.

Our terminological choices were guided by the aim of producing a text that preserves a strong sense of the local setting without sacrificing elegance of expression. One term that we kept in its original form is *kabar*. Houat offers his own footnote for this word, describing it as being of Malagasy origin, and suggesting that it is related to the term *kava* used in Polynesia. Meaning an assembly or conference, it is used in the novel to refer to the escapees' conspiratorial meetings. This translation is intended primarily to serve as a work of literature, not as a work of literary scholarship, so we leave it to more qualified researchers to assess the validity of Houat's etymology. Our task is not to lay bare all the intricacies and nuances that undergird this novel, but to present such mysteries at face value. That said, we have made every effort to ensure that the names of landforms, plants, animals, and other natural phenomena are rendered accurately, despite the many risks of confusion incurred by inconsistencies in nineteenth-century nomenclatures.

We found it necessary to strike a balance between conveying that which was common to various global manifestations of enslavement in the nineteenth century and depicting the particularity of practices and constructs specific to the French colonies in the Indian Ocean. For example, some methods of punishment and torture were used throughout the colonial world, while others were not. The device that Houat refers to as the *bloc* or *courbari* is functionally identical to the "stocks" used in the English-speaking world, so we have used this recognizable English term. On the other hand, the practice of tying a person down to four stakes, one at each wrist and ankle, in order to maximize the humiliation and suffering of flogging, seems to be a uniquely French innovation in cruelty. Therefore, we have chosen to refer to this practice by its original name, the *quatre-piquets*.

While the use of such borrowed words highlights the particularity of the context, it also seemed important to evoke the substantial parallels between French colonial plantation slavery and that practiced in the American South. For this reason, we have chosen to use some key words from the

American lexicon. The most noteworthy examples of these are "driver" and "overseer." The French term *commandeur* refers to an individual (often drawn from the ranks of the enslaved Africans themselves) placed in a position of immediate authority over a group of enslaved people, tasked with directing their labor and meting out punishments. It appears that the nearest equivalent on the U.S. plantation would be a "slave driver" or simply "driver." At a position of higher authority is the figure known as a *régisseur* and sometimes as an *économe*, more or less equivalent to the "overseer." We have therefore chosen to use the terms "driver" and "overseer," emphasizing the fundamental similarities among the power structures at play in the different historical manifestations of plantation slavery.

The most complex and politically fraught terminological decision had to do with the French term *nègre*. While Houat frequently uses the term *noir* to refer to a Black person, he sometimes also uses "nègre" in a neutral, non-derogatory manner. Houat himself was a person of mixed race and would have been considered Black in his time. We have mostly opted to use the term "Negro" as the nearest possible equivalent to the French "nègre." This choice is by no means straightforward. Like the French equivalent, the word "Negro" was used in the nineteenth century by Whites and Blacks alike. However, it was not the term of choice among mid-century American abolitionists; rather, the preferred term at the time was "colored." In his *Narrative of the Life of Frederick Douglass, an American Slave* (1845), the most prominent Black American abolitionist used the word "colored" much more frequently than he did "Negro." However, in his 1855 work *My Bondage and My Freedom*, Douglass used the word "Negro" practically interchangeably with "colored." The term "colored" presents its own disadvantages as a translation of the French "nègre," mainly because in many contexts—particularly South Africa—it denotes mixed race rather than Blackness *per se*.

The term "Negro" later went on to become a preferred term for self-designation among Black Americans, partially due to the endorsement of the word by W. E. B. Du Bois and Booker T. Washington around the turn of the twentieth century. Similarly, starting in the 1920s, the francophone Négritude movement led by Aimé Césaire and Leopold Senghor sought to reclaim the word "nègre" and turn it into a badge of honor. All told, despite some similarities, the asymmetry between the usages of the French term and its English cognate means that no perfect equivalence is possible. Nevertheless, considering the need for a compromise, and hoping to avoid overburdening the text with italicized borrowings, we have mostly opted to use "Negro" to translate the term "nègre." We recognize that the word now appears dated and, generally speaking, offensive. Nevertheless, the task of historical translation requires us to engage with history in an attitude of honest curiosity. Language evolves over time, and words take on new meanings and connotations. Houat used the term "nègre" in much the same way that Douglass did "Negro," and that is the sense in which the word is presented in this translation.

On two occasions in the novel, a White character utters the term "nègre" with racist contempt. For these instances, rather than using the supremely slanderous variant now known as the "N-word," we have decided to use the original French term. Like any literary work, a translation is always situated in its own historical circumstances. Such circumstances must be taken into account if a translation is to achieve its purposes, with particular attention to the sensibilities of the intended audience. In the case of *The Maroons*, we hope to offer a version of Houat's novel that conveys the author's revolutionary, abolitionist, humanitarian messages to contemporary readers. The desire to avoid alienating readers is not the only rationale for using the French word "nègre" in those instances when it is used as a slur. This practice, known as "zero translation," is most useful when certain conditions are present: when the term is strongly culturally marked in a manner that makes any true equivalence impossible, and when the meaning of the term will be easily deducible from its form (i.e., if it is a cognate or otherwise recognizable) and its context. The term "nègre," when used as a slur, meets these criteria. It captures connotations of race and caste that were specific to the French colonial context; it is in some ways broader than the English term "Negro" because it can cover the same semantic range as both that word and its more derogatory variant.

Beyond these terminological considerations, we have sought to present the book's central themes of abolition, escape, and revolution with the same lucid fervor found in the original. The author's prescience in his treatment of these themes is noteworthy. One of the most intriguing aspects of this work is the way in which it addresses the prospect and reality of race mixing. In the loving relationship between Frême and Marie, the text presents an endorsement of interracial marriage. Later, in the form of a powerful dream sequence, the narrative paints a picture of a glorious future in which distinctions of race and caste have disappeared, with all the races of humanity fused into one. This immediately brings to mind the theories of the early twentieth-century Mexican cultural theorist José Vasconcelos, whose 1925 book *La Raza Cósmica* (*The Cosmic Race*) asserts a similar vision of utopian harmony grounded in generalized racial convergence. The idea that biological race mixing would inevitably make racism and racial exploitation obsolete may seem naïve from a contemporary perspective, but in the context of *The Maroons* it deserves to be recognized as a radical departure from the exclusionary attitudes about racial purity that were prevalent at the time. Such attitudes are depicted in the novel itself, in the form of the harassment Marie and Frême endure from the White settlers. In translating such scenes of cruelty, as well as the passages evoking the possibilities of change, we have sought to avoid euphemism and provide a clear, faithful rendition so that the contrast between the depravity of reality and the grandeur of the dream remains just as striking as in the original.

It has been an immense honor to collaborate with Aqiil Gopee, Shenaz Patel, and the brilliant team at Restless Books to bring this novel to an English-speaking readership. We extend our sincere gratitude to Kaiama Glover, John McWhorter, William Hart, Nadia Horning, and Shanta Lee for taking the time to offer advice on linguistic matters.

One of the loftiest purposes for translation is that of exposing worthy authors to a new audience. Perhaps this translation will contribute to further revelations about the extent of revolutionary consciousness among the enslaved populations of the Indian Ocean and help bring long overdue recognition to Louis Timagène Houat as a political thinker and literary writer. With a spirit of humility and curiosity, we offer this translation to our readers in the hope that it will spark new conversations about race, rights, history, and freedom.

JEFFREY DITEMAN

THE
MAROONS

I

Collusion

A LONG TIME had passed since the tropical sun disappeared beneath the edge of the Indian Ocean. The night, ordinarily so clear and beautiful, stirring the shadows with cooling breezes under the scorching tropical sky, was now overcast, with nary a star to be seen.

The Negro had just finished his long day of toil. He was ready to lie down on his ragged straw mat and get some rest. It was the only piece of furniture that adorned his hut. On the sugar plantations, the terrible, hoarse voice of the slave drivers had given way to silence. A distant rooster began hollering its nightsong, signaling the time of rest. Apart from the clipped, monotonous shrieks of some stonechat—a solitary bird similar to the lark—leaving its isolated branch and soaring steeply into the sky, nothing disturbed the peace that had settled over the countryside.

At that time of night, in the year 1833, four barely clothed individuals were leaving the same colonial residence. On tiptoe and each taking a different path, they began crossing a vast sugarcane field. Its broad green carpet extended to the foot of the Salazes, Bourbon Island's tallest mountain range.

The men, except for one born in the colony, hailed from the great island of Madagascar. They had been taken from their country and sold as commodities of the slave trade to the Whites. One belonged to the Ovas tribe, also known as the Amboilames, who appear to be of White and Malay ancestry. Another was of the Antacimes, known for their Tahitian hue and features. Like most Malagasy peoples, they had been defeated and conquered by the very same Amboilames, led by the renowned chief Radama. The third, finally, belonged to the Sçacalaves, descended from the Cafres and the Arabs. Despite the Ovas' relentless wars against the Sçacalaves, they had never been able to bring them to their knees. Now, all four of them belonged to the same master. They were equals in the grips of misery, fated to curse the very same chains.

They had been walking that way for almost an hour, moving stealthily like ostriches. After each step, they would halt and listen, careful to avoid any human encounter that could jeopardize their plans. They chose the darkest, least trodden paths and ultimately reached a sort of palisade hedge bristling with razor-sharp thorns—a fence planted with aloeswood, prickly pear, and sappanwood, as was customary on the boundaries of colonial settlements.

How reckless of them to attempt breaching such a dangerous barrier, especially in pitch darkness! But they were determined, and dropped to all fours. Crawling and wriggling on their bellies when necessary, they sought the clearest path through the thicket, leaving shreds of tattered rags and even bits of flesh behind. Yet, their perseverance prevailed, and they successfully crossed the formidable barricade, emerging onto a vast plain—the kind known in the colonies as a savannah.

There, alone and isolated, stood a huge tamarisk tree that loomed like a great phantom before them. It was, so to speak, the guardian angel of that land. It towered over the savannah, its bushy branches sprawling and twisting around, forming a massive cone that, in the daytime, cast a shadow that even the sweltering sun could not pierce. Black men sometimes wandered across this barren expanse. Overtaken by the heat and exhaustion, they would lie in its shade, offering their heartfelt gratitude for its providence.

When they reached that gigantic tree, the men stopped, one by one, as if responding to a secret signal. Beneath its branches, they found themselves concealed from view—the perfect vantage point to survey the surrounding landscape. They blended seamlessly into the shadows in a fashion befitting their objective, the night lending them her dreary majesty.

"Yes!" exclaimed the Sçacalave in a thoughtful voice, as if he were continuing, rather than beginning, a conversation. "Our time as slaves is up, brothers! Enough is enough!"

"Enough, yes, enough is enough!" repeated the others in muffled unison.

"After all," continued the first one with unrelenting passion, "what's death to us, brothers? What's to fear about it? What have we got to leave behind, anyway? Joy? Rest? Happiness? Vile mockeries! Hard work, all the time, always kneeling before the master; beatings, misery, endless servitude, there it is, yes, our truth, our reality, yes, our share in this world! I curse this life! Yes, I curse it because for me it's like being in the furnace of the volcano that crackles there, over the mount! And also because sleep, the good lord of master and slave alike, flees from me now, like a damned maroon! But even if it did come back, I would spurn it like an unwelcome guest! Let's not be fooled by our suffering. The Black man who sleeps in the yoke is like an animal wallowing in the mud. He is a wretched being, my brothers: he may groan, but he will never escape the claws that clutch him . . .

"The memory is still fresh, plaguing my mind . . . that dreadful moment when they tore me away from my *grande-terre*, my home. I had to leave everything behind! The merciless slavers shackled me in chains and tossed me into the hold of a ship like I was nothing more than a bale of sugarcane or cotton. Oh! I wonder how, as I began to endure the horror of my humiliation, I was able to contain, to restrain, to suppress the urge to revolt? Why didn't I take my own life, strangle myself right in front of those barbaric smugglers? My mother! Yes, my mother! Seeing her chained right beside me left me paralyzed, disarmed! Regardless of my strength or weakness, I knew I had to survive, if not for myself, then for her . . . I figured that with time, through sheer habit and willpower, I would be able to suppress or obliterate my true self, stifle the cries of my conscience, forsaking notions of freedom, country, and family, resigning myself to the fate of a slave! Alas! What use was that ordeal? Why did I patiently endure such bondage? I saw my mother collapse under the driver's whip, her body covered in blood. I found her lifeless, murdered! And I could neither save her nor seek revenge! Oh, brothers, we are more than mere beasts of burden pulling carts. Despite everything, a spark of humanity, an instinct, still lingers within . . . and that instinct made the cries in my heart even stronger, cries I couldn't let out, even though every injury intensified them . . . instead of submitting or

7

becoming tame, I have transformed into a true scourge! My heart brims with abhorrence for slavery and hatred for the masters' race, so much so that it overflows, oh brothers, surpassing my own cowardice, driving my desire for vengeance!"

He paused, as if wrestling with unspeakable emotions. He then went on, more calmly:

"Of course, the master's brutality has not increased; but, brothers, could it really? Is there any spot left on our body that a finger could graze without feeling the whip's furrow? I won't speak of the house dog—the master's friend and loyal companion—but what about the stable horse? Isn't it treated a thousand times better than us? The horse has its attendants, many of our own people, catering to its needs. It strolls and rests, feasting on plentiful grass and grain, shining with pride and contentment. But what about us, brothers? Day and night, we toil, endure beatings, and suffer in misery . . . our bodies flayed, our bones exposed, and we starve as we bow our heads low, our legs trembling with shame before our fellow men. Yet, every day, they hypocritically speak of our welfare! What welfare is that? Where is it? Do you see it? If we wish to stretch our legs for a moment, abandon our meager sleep and take a short walk outside the workshop, can we? Isn't the constabulary stationed there, right at the boundary, eager to pounce like a wolf? If they catch us, we are bound, beaten with the flat of their sabers, and tossed into jail to spend the night in a cell. The next day, there we are, early in the morning, tied to a post at the grand market, stripped naked, lashed until we bleed, and then, as if that weren't enough, we are forced to sweep the streets with a chain around our necks!

"And yet, they have the audacity to accuse us of gluttony! What do they feed us? Mere morsels of cassava! They fling the scraps at us as if we were lowly swine! Brothers, isn't it true that they only feed us to keep us from dying? And when, in our desperate hunger, we chance upon a small ear of corn, what torment do they inflict upon us? It is the very corn we toil to plant! We irrigate the fields with our own sweat! If we survive the beatings, they twist our limbs, tie us up, loop wet twine around our thumbs, and leave us suspended from a tree for hours on end. They fasten giant iron collars around our necks. Our heads or feet are wedged between two beams in the stocks. I mean, would they not go as far as muzzling us, or pulling out our teeth, just to prevent us from eating some fallen fruit?* Enough is enough, brothers! It's time for courage! It's time to rattle the chains, to avenge ourselves as men! Let's revolt! This is our battle cry, our last labor! Let's revolt! Let's loot the workshops! Let's

* Such atrocities may seem unimaginable, but regrettably, they are all too real. Recent news has shed light on the recurring acts of horror that were committed in Cayenne. [*Author's footnote*]

9

eradicate them all at once! Let's blast across the island like a cyclone! Yes, let's get revenge! Let's burn the fields that were fertilized with our pain, let's destroy the houses we built for them! Let their ruins litter the earth, and may this very earth, swamped with our sweat, be fattened with the blood of our tormentors!"

A low moan, like a dull echo, rose to welcome these words of vengeance. The Antacime then began his speech:

"Our Sçacalave brother has recalled things that make tears fall on the heart. I can't talk like him, my tongue is slow to catch up with what I feel inside. So speaking of what has been done to me . . . feels impossible, but I will never forget . . . I was a young boy, still just a child, when they snatched me from my homeland. I had been tending to our oxen in the fields, and as I started my journey back home, out of nowhere, somebody seized me. I fought and screamed, but they gagged me and kicked me. I was scared to death. Finally, they tied my arms behind my back, lifted me like a log, and quickly took me far, far away."

"Oh! So much pain!"

"And you understand my tears and my despair . . . thinking of my family and seeing myself turned into a slave! On the ship, they untied my hands only to throw me into a barrel with several others. Later, I realized that many of us were crammed into such barrels, a ploy to conceal their illicit activities. I cannot find words to describe the torment we endured, my brothers, confined in that coffin-like space, trapped amidst the sick and the deceased. We suffered from searing heat, insatiable thirst, and agonizing hunger, with nothing to eat or drink but filthy, rotten things . . . "

"Oh! It's horrible!" one of them interjected. "I know this all too well, because, on board, they forced me to consume the flesh of our comrades. And when another ship gave us chase, they threw my brother and others, still alive, into the sea!"

"I'm not sure," continued the Antacime, "what they fed us. But the meat we were given was truly dreadful, absolutely repugnant . . . Just the thought of it makes me want to retch . . . As for our comrades, I can't say for sure if they tossed them into the sea while they were still alive. I was too young to fully comprehend, but it's quite possible they did, considering they had no qualms about using crowbars to brutally beat anyone who dared to peek out from their barrel."

"What! So they would murder a drowning man for nothing but his desire to breathe?"

"Precisely!"

"Oh! God cannot forget that!"

"Neither can I, brothers . . . for I still vividly recall two of those wretched ones, their faces beaten to a pulp, as they fell upon us, writhing in their final moments, bleeding all over . . . We were stuck in there for days on end, and after what felt

11

like an eternity, we finally arrived at Bourbon Island. They treated us like dead bodies, swiftly piling us onto overcrowded pirogues that brought us ashore, where we were dumped onto the pebbles . . . I felt so weak, and yet they kept striking me to force me to stand and continue walking until I grew dizzy and collapsed. When I regained consciousness, I found myself lying in a large warehouse. I longed for that peaceful sleep to last forever . . . it had momentarily eased the pain . . . but ever since then, I've suffered so much, I have so keenly felt the misery of life as a slave! Oh, brothers, they beat and whip you . . . if the beatings don't kill you, hunger surely will . . . and it hurts, that much is true, but when they take your wife, your grandchildren, and sell them at the public auction . . . Oh! That is much more than pain! The body feels nothing at all, and yet, my God! The torture drives you mad and you wish you could murder somebody, or have somebody murder you . . . " He lowered his voice, and continued:

"'Listen here!' said the master to little Kaïla the other day. She avoided his gaze, as the master's eyes had an ominous glow to them. 'Come on! Come here, my little Negress!' Kaïla lowered her head, and would not obey. 'Get over here at once! That's an order!' And seeing that Kaïla was more scared of whatever he had in mind than of him, the master told his men to grab her. After having had her beaten and her dress lifted, he had her head shaved and threw her into a cell. You remember, long ago, Ravana the beautiful, with a big collar around her neck, with barely any hair on her head—same fate. We can expect no justice, no quarter from masters who can do whatever they please. Whenever they murder someone, and somebody speaks up, they lie and blame the plague, not their bloody hands. That's what happened to Namcimoine and Songol, and many others. To be honest, brothers, we're at fault too. We're complicit in our own misery. Things would have changed a long time ago had slaves not been the way they are. Look, two days ago Koutkel's grandchild picked up a mango—and as we know there are plenty on the estate. He was hungry, so he ate it. The master was informed and soon enough, at his command, one Black held him while another beat him, and the poor child ended up covered in bruises . . . And then, who digs the holes to make room for the bellies of pregnant women that the master orders to be whipped? Who trusses us up and straps us to the *quatre-piquets*? Who monitors and reports everything we do? And who executes every vile and barbaric act the master commands? Oh! Yes, brothers, the Blacks are complicit. They flatter the very masters who ill-treat them, and support them against their own interests. Instead of coming together as comrades, instead of refusing to assist the masters, to stop them from committing further harm, instead of gathering, of awakening as men and telling them: 'We have hands and feet and blood like you, and we do not want to be trod upon anymore, to be brought to our knees like this.'

"Now that, in order to try to do that very thing, we've met here *en Kabar*,* my lonely heart is happy, and it sings. But if we do succeed, brothers, let's not plunder, let's not murder anyone—that would anger our good God—we are mighty enough to achieve freedom without killing. And those fields, those houses, why should we burn and destroy them? They have committed no crime, and we might ourselves need them, when we are free . . . Yes, brothers; without shedding blood, and without plundering this island, we can have our uprising.

"Here is my plan: after we are done discussing, and after we have agreed on everything, we will split up. We will each visit different estates and go talk to friends, win the hearts of groups, and gather assemblies. When the big day finally comes, we shall all rise together. There will be as many of us as the eyes can see. Nobody will dare resist us. Together, we shall all say: *we are free!* And we shall be free. The masters will still live in the country, but their lives will not be worth

---

* The word *Kabar*, which has been creolized in Bourbon Island, comes from the Malagasy language and carries the same meaning as the word *kava* used by certain communities in Oceania: assembly, reunion, deliberation, conference. The linguistic connection between these two languages, along with the similarities in skin tone, hair, and physical characteristics between the Malagasy people and the Polynesians, provide support for the notion that these two groups share a common ancestry. [*Author's footnote*]

more than ours. Otherwise, we will give them ships so they can leave. Here, I have told you what I feel, the best I could. Now let another speak."

The Sçacalave wanted to respond, but someone said it was the Câpre's turn to talk, so he yielded and instead gestured for his Creole companion to express his thoughts. After a brief moment of hesitation, the latter positioned himself in the midst of the group and began:

"When I first set foot in this place, my brothers, I believed that we would never have a chance to speak, that our voices would be silenced and our only role would be to listen and obey. But now, you wish to hear my words! Well then, I shall let my tongue speak, even though it is lined with thorns. I have remained silent for far too long, and my heart would weep if I did not unburden it now . . .

"However, I will not recount every trial and hardship I have endured. What purpose would it serve, my brothers? We are all too familiar with the atrocities of slavery, and revisiting my personal torment will not extinguish the flames of our suffering. It would only ignite them further.

"Let's focus on the matter at hand. You want revolution?"

"Yes! Yes!"

"Well then, I too, brothers! We have endured far too much . . . But what can I say? I worry that we may lack . . . Our Antacime and Sçacalave brothers have spoken of unity, of a grand uprising . . . but I must apologize, I find it difficult to trust . . . "

"What do you mean? Are we not all trapped in the same hell?"

"I do not deny that, brothers, but as you have acknowledged, we do not all see eye to eye, and some among us align with the masters. By conspiring, we run the risk of further dividing our own ranks. One, two, maybe three Blacks may join our cause, but the fourth could turn out to be a false brother, and betray us . . . "

"Betray us?!"

"Yes, betray us! And then, how dreadful! We will be captured before we can even raise a finger, before we can even loosen the first link of our chains . . . We will be enslaved once again, and the blood of our bravest comrades will flow . . . "

"Let it flow! Our blood doesn't even belong to us! What do we have to lose?"

"I understand, brothers, I understand that for us, death is sweeter, preferable to life. But why let our deaths be in vain? Painful and dishonorable deaths . . . I am simply thinking aloud. Perhaps we should assess our comrades . . . "

"They want revolution!"

"We have been speaking to everyone—"

"No one will betray us, we are united!"

"If that is so, then let's revolt!"

"Let's revolt!"

"They hack us to pieces with their sabers . . . crush us with their cannonballs—"

"No matter! Let's march!"

"We can march, as you say, and go even further, and one day, there we will be, free! But that is not all, brothers . . . This island is too small . . . France will send warships to fight us . . . we'll be burned, killed, forced back into slavery, and then everything will be far worse! Listen to me: from what I have heard, in France and England, the great nations of the Whites, there are men, children of God, who think like us. They pray for us and argue that, despite our black skin, we are White, just like them. They have been pleading with the King and the Queen, imploring them to release us, to grant us our freedom . . . "

"Grant us our freedom!"

"Indeed, brothers! So let us be patient for just a while longer. It will happen any time now. Every day brings us closer to our salvation. The Whites here are against it, of course. But it doesn't matter: their leaders are there, not here, and it is they who will bring us our freedom. And then, we will finally be given our own shacks, our own patches of land, our own vegetables and fowl. We'll work when we have to, but for ourselves, not for them. We will not be beaten, we will be the masters of our own bodies. Our wives and children will be by our side, with us. Our lives will be fulfilled, and we won't be sad anymore . . .

"Oh! Brothers, let's not do anything foolish! Let's await this glad tiding, that thing called *emancipation*. In the meantime, given the cruel treatment we endure on the plantation, let us gather our meager belongings and escape from the master. We will become maroons and seek refuge in the Salazes. My grandfather has been living there for many years, evading capture. He may even be a leader by now and will surely be overjoyed to see us. There, we'll get food and drink to our heart's content, because they have it all: syrup, honey, arrack, strawberries, potatoes, palm kernels, mangoes, bananas, gobies, shrimp, eels, blackbirds, shearwaters, chicken, pigs, brown goats, and thousands and thousands of other things in great quantities. We will be as good as free. We will do what we please! What say you, brothers?"

"That is all very good!" answered the Amboilame after a moment of silence. He replaced his comrade at the center of the circle, and continued: "But it will not do. I have been a maroon before. I know the Salazes. They're beyond anything you can imagine. They're divine! Oh, they're sublime, absolutely magnificent! But, alas . . . They do not belong to us! Furthermore, while I agree with what you have said, my Creole brother, there is something else to consider. There are advantages, there is a certain degree of freedom, yes.

But there is also evil: danger lurks. We should not forget the scouts, the wicked little Whites that they hire to hunt you down like dogs, and to whom they pay so many francs. I have heard that they pay them based on the limbs they bring in: a price per leg, per arm, of the poor Blacks that they slaughter."

"Bunch of wicked little Whites!"

"Oh! They are sophisticated people, cunning and skilled watchdogs, let's give them that, brothers! They can track you down wherever you are, chase you along any mountain, any cliff, and find you even in the most remote corners, the smallest crevices of the earth . . . And beware of the hounds! Beware of their guns!"

"Zounds! It's no good . . . We can run, but we can't outrun a bullet!"

"Indeed, it's no laughing matter! Day and night, we must tread lightly, keep our ears sharp, and our eyes peeled! We must become one with the hare, the deer, the stonechat, and the lizard, and like them, hop from rock to rock, skip from ridge to ridge! Otherwise, they will catch you, brothers, and if they don't kill you, they'll roll you up like a cigar and take you to the master . . . And as if to say 'serves you right,' that brute will sear your behind with a hundred lashes and marinate your wounds in vinegar, salt, and chili pepper. What a sight! You will be restrained, tied to the large boulder at the estate . . . Grinding corn on the millstone for months and months, like a wretched thing, under the sun, buffeted by the rain and the wind. Is that what you want, brothers?"

"Oh!" exclaimed the Antacime. "Thank you! Always fearful, always on guard . . . constantly facing death . . . and at the end of the day seized, if not gunned down, chained again, and you're twice as much of a captive! Oh! No, we wouldn't want that . . . there is no good in that . . . Misfortune upon misfortune, maybe it's better to stay at the master's and let our misery consume us!"

"No, absolutely not!" continued the Amboilame, in a self-assured voice. He slapped his forehead and declared: "Because I have come up with my own idea. We blather too much. We keep talking. One says this . . . the other says that . . . Farfabé agrees, Grangousier disagrees. We have no clue what to do or how to proceed. Yet, none of us wants to slide his neck back into the collar, none of us wants to shovel his way back into slavery . . .

"Let us listen to each other, brothers, and we will find agreement . . . *One*, we will not stay at the master's . . . *Two*, we will not be betrayed or sold . . . *Three*, we won't rebel . . . *Four*, we won't shed any blood . . . *Five*, we won't go into the Salazes . . . *Six*, finally, we will be free, and citizens of our own country . . . "

"How so! How so!" exclaimed the others, their eyes round in astonishment.

20

"Surely," continued the Amboilame, pointing to the sea, "our country, our *grande-terre*, is not here, is it?"

"Alas, indeed!" answered one of them. "But we cannot tread the sky, and the sea is too deep for our feet to reach . . ."

"Well!" said the Amboilame. "A man does not only have feet to walk, he also has fins and wings when the need arises . . . Listen. Do you know of the *Little Cove*, and do you know what that thing is called, that treads on the sea?"

"A ship!"

"Yes, a ship . . . It is the vessel that brought us here, and shall be the vessel that carries us back, our salvation . . . Therefore, brothers, I have chosen, in my mind, a pretty little boat that they haul up onto the land at night, there in the harbor . . . it has oars like fins, and sails like wings: it's all we will need for our voyage.

"Right now it's too late for us to begin. We have to get back, and spend the morrow at the master's. We shall then gather provisions wherever we can, then, at night, when everybody is asleep, we will sneak out of the workshop, moving slowly, slowly, just like today, until we reach the little boat. Once the coast is clear, quick! We'll cut the rope, and whack! We're on the water, leaving slavery in our wake, leaving behind the fearful and those who betray their brethren . . . Then, we begin paddling. If the wind is right, we unfurl the sails.

21

We speed across the sea . . . We cross the reefs, continuing our swift traverse . . . And behold, we find ourselves in our homeland! Yes, brothers, in our own country, guzzling fresh, delicious cow's milk, indulging in nourishing rice and ripe bananas, hunting with our bows and spears, running, dancing in the field, working, sleeping as much as we want, in our huts, embracing our freedom, our property, our family! Oh, brothers! Would you refuse such bliss?"

"Refuse?!" cried out the Sçacalave. "What say you, brothers? How could we possibly refuse our freedom, our country, our family? I asked for revolt and revenge; my speech echoed what was inside my heart. Did I pour my soul into those words just to become a liar and remain enslaved? But then someone says the plan is impossible. I keep listening . . . If you wish to try something else, I won't object. Although I doubt your plan will succeed, brother, I will concede and follow your lead . . . I know we are not sailors, and I am well aware that the gales of the sea, much like our masters, show no mercy. But I would rather sink to the bottom of the ocean than toil in chains any longer . . . "

"Me too!" exclaimed the Antacime, his voice choked with emotion.

"As for me," answered the Câpre dolefully, "I will pray to the Lord for your safe travels, but I cannot follow you . . . Your country is not mine."

"Nonsense! Are you not our brother? Our home will be yours. You'll be better off than in this country where you were born a slave . . . "

"Oh! Yes, I thank you, brothers . . . but the voyage remains uncertain . . . and I need to go to the Salazes to see my grandfather . . . "

"Well, as you wish, Creole brother . . . But you might well change your mind come tomorrow," reasoned one of the three Malagasies. They exchanged a few more words among themselves before parting in the stillest of silences.

II

The Plantation

NEARLY TWO HOURS had passed since the silent parting of our four companions. A milky glow, the gauze of dawn, had begun to appear, vaguely wafting over the edges of the Orient.

Like a sylph heralding the coming of day, the white-tailed tropicbird had left its nest. It sang the tidings of daybreak, carrying its melody from leaf to leaf, from branch to branch.

The blackbird was also waking up. Its voice softly echoed across the morning winds as it replicated the cheerful report, as diligently as the honeybee suckling the treasures nestled inside granadillas and rose-apples.

It was spring, but spring, summer, winter, autumn, what does it matter in the tropical island's climate? Heat, fruits, flowers, and lush greenery abound year-round.

The day kept stretching and swelling. It lifted a sweet, pleasant, invigorating, blissful, soft breeze that drifted, dense with fragrances, inducing in its wake an ineffable drunkenness. It felt like the divine breath of creation and of life itself!

The sun was about to rise. Shimmering clouds, like seraphs, proclaimed its coming. Everything seemed to hold its breath in anticipation. Finally, as it burst forth in a blaze of light, revealing its radiant countenance, a general symphony erupted.

The air was filled with the droning wings of the golden fly; the waxbill's little jolting, chromatic shriek; the canary's arias and flourishes; and the turtledove's cooing, like the serenade of a young girl in love.

Everything was singing: the waterfall, as it cascaded down the mountain; the pristine stream, caressing the green grass; the droplet of dew, shimmering over leaves and beaming inside flowers; the butterfly, frolicking and fluttering its colorful wings over each perfumed corolla; the swaying palm tree, its emerald fronds swishing in the breeze; the guava tree and its myriad pink blooms; the birds, the insects, the trees, the whole of nature—yes, everything was music to the ears and a delight for the eyes, everything was expressing bliss in this paradise, except, of course, for the miserable Negro . . .

Alas! Indeed, only him! For this beautiful and blessed hour brings him no joy, but instead snatches him away from the tender dreams of the night and plunges him into the harsh reality of his doomed fate. It serves as a cruel reminder that he is a slave, destined for another day of labor, exhaustion, and brutal beatings. It is the sorrowful hour when his voice rises to the sky, not in prayer, but in lament! It is the wretched hour when his body contorts in agony as he endures the lashings at the *quatre-piquets*! It is the hour when the master, after receiving reports of the previous day's work, unleashes terrible punishments—his own twisted way of greeting the sunrise!

Now, let us take a closer look at the landscape before us. Just ahead, past some master's beautiful house, which overlooks a grand avenue adorned with pineapple plants, stands a bustling sugar mill with crushing rollers operating at full steam. Next to it is a field of sugar beets, swaying their innumerable flower stems and delicate plumes and stretching off into the distance as far as the eye can see. Their constant motion gives them the appearance of a formidable army encamped between the mountain and the estate.

To the right, we behold symmetrical rows of clove trees and nutmeg trees adorned with purplish nuts. They stand firmly in a broad, elongated expanse of soil, flanked by storehouses, barns, and small slave huts, built with thatch and leaves. A line of towering tropical trees forms a protective hedge, separating this area from the sprawling cocoa trees, distinguished by their long, red, ribbed fruits. On the other side are flourishing coffee bushes, each adorned with clusters of ripe berries that weigh heavily on their branches.

To the left, there are a few straw huts nestled among green hedges. We then encounter the sheepcotes, stables, and henhouses as the vine- and flower-covered alleys unfurl before us. Further on, a diverse array of gardens emerges, leading to the grand orchard divided by a branch of the river. In sum, we are on one of those colonial estates that are so rich and varied in sights and produce that they cannot quite be described.

However, let us now turn our gaze amidst this abundance and opulence, and behold the wretched state of the slaves—naked, emaciated, and starved—forced to toil like beasts of burden! Our attention is drawn to the *platform*, at the heart of the estate, where three men are tied up, their bellies pressed against the earth, their limbs outstretched. With long whips in hand, others relentlessly lash them, driven by the menacing commands of the overseer and the master. Blood spills forth! Flesh is torn asunder! Yet not a cry, not a moan escapes their lips! Is there, inside of these men, something mightier than pain? Undoubtedly, within their hearts, myriad emotions intertwine, granting them solace and fortitude in the face of their torment. Otherwise, they would not be enduring such torture in silence, watching, with the fortitude of martyrs, the gates of an unseen heaven opening right in front of them!

But the beatings have ceased. Where are they taking those three unfortunate souls, whom we have already recognized as three of our comrades from the night before? It's the worst place imaginable—a dungeon, built behind the sugar mill, now opens ominously before them! It is a dismal cell, shrouded in darkness and reeking of decay. But it is not enough to entomb them—they are locked in the stocks, their feet clamped between two large planks, which, purposefully designed to inflict such torture, serve as the resident devils of this infernal abode! Pain married to despair! And yet, not a word has yet escaped from their tortured breasts! Finally, the perpetrators of the master's orders depart. The Amboilame breaks the silence and, addressing his two companions, says, "I'm sorry, brothers!" with pain in his voice, and as if he were himself either immune to, or guilty of their affliction. He goes on, "Yes, I'm sorry! I was wrong to urge you to return to this cursed plantation . . . "

The Antacime paused and let out a deep sigh—a gesture that conveyed more in that moment than any words could express. The Sçacalave did not seem to have heard anything, but a stream of muffled sounds came out of his mouth, among which certain words could be discerned: "Blood . . . cell . . . stocks . . . revenge!" This last word was proclaimed so vehemently, in such a roaring tone, that the Amboilame felt the need to calm his friend down. He said:

"Yes, brothers, I was wrong . . . but who could have foreseen that the despicable overseer would notice our absence and inform the master?"

The Sçacalave, once more, appeared oblivious, and sharply repeated: "Blood . . . cell . . . stocks . . . revenge!" He added, in a jeering, rageful tone, "Never mind! No revenge! Let's keep bowing down and kissing the feet of the masters who slaughter us!"

"Yes, they are butchers," said the Amboilame, still speaking with measured reserve, "but, brothers, let's be patient: we will break free from their grasp. Whether it's today, tomorrow, or someday in the future, we shall ultimately achieve . . . "

"Alas!" interjected the Antacime, his face contorted in regret. "Our Creole brother made a wiser choice by not coming back here with us! He wasn't beaten, nor is he confined in a cell or the stocks! He's free in the woods! He's happier than any of us!"

"You should not say such things, Antacime brother!" answered the Amboilame in a soft, yet admonishing tone. "Understand that our Creole brother is now a maroon, and he might face the threat of being killed or arrested! Yes, we have been beaten, confined in cells, and put in stocks, but what's done is done. While the threat of such a fate still looms over him, along with that of other greater misfortunes, we, for the time being, have nothing further to fear. We're back where we started, that's all. Because, once we escape from here, we'll resume our initial plan, and let them try to catch us this time! The little boat still waits for us, and we'll sail away . . . "

As he finished his sentence, they heard the sound of footsteps and the rattling of keys from outside. The Amboilame fell silent.

What had become of the Black Creole now? Was he truly in a better place?

III

Maroonage

AS WE HAVE SEEN, the Câpre held different intentions than his comrades, and did not feel the need to accompany them after their meeting at the great tamarisk. While the three Malagasies, who had agreed to go by the Amboilame's plan, were walking back to the plantation, expecting to stay there for only one more day, the Câpre had embarked on a solitary journey toward the Salazes. He did not follow them, perhaps having foreseen the dreadful fate that awaited them. True to his word during their collusion, he had become a maroon.

Between their gathering point and the nearest foot of the Salazes lay a distance of approximately four to five kilometers, as the crow flies. At first glance, this initial stretch seemed relatively short. However, it took our fugitive two hours to cover it. It is not that he was in no hurry to leave the savannah, nor that he got distracted along the way; if anything, the place was too open for him to wish to stay there for longer than necessary. But the route was not straight, and became more and more crooked and difficult to tread, until soon there remained no path at all. He found himself surrounded by thick brushwood and thorny thickets that he had to navigate. Treacherous streams meandered around the hills, adding to the obstacles he faced. By the time he reached the daunting base of the mountains, dawn had already broken.

He had to tap into his last reserves of strength, summon all the courage within him because it was clear that the worst was yet to come. Despite his exhaustion, he didn't retreat or shrink back at the sight of the towering giant before him. Instead, he grappled with this formidable mass of rock, which stood like a pointed pyramid, and began to climb using his hands and belly as much as his feet. To an onlooker, he would have appeared like an ant struggling upon a colossal sugarloaf, with the crucial difference being that for him, the slightest misstep could result in a horrifying death. His only means of ascending and maintaining balance above the abyss were patches of sparse grass and irregularly spaced fractures in the rock.

But there came a moment when even these fragile supports became elusive—an awful moment when the mountain abruptly curved, forming an elbow-like bend, and presented nothing but a sheer, vertical face looming above him! How could he possibly climb this? What could he grasp on to? He felt like going back down, retracing his steps. But to do so, without the fear, the certainty of falling, he would have needed eyes on his toes . . . How else could he find his way back? His hands dared not leave the places where they had hooked themselves, and his feet, desperate for crevices to step into, swam in vain against the cliff . . .

Thus suspended, unable to climb up or down, and supported by nothing but a proverbial strand of hair at such a terrifying height, he was suddenly consumed by the haunting thought of plummeting to his demise, crushed to a pulp at the base of the mountain!

His entire body turned slick with sweat, his breath grew shallow and laborious, his frantic heartbeat constricted his chest—he could hardly breathe . . .

His sweaty fingers were beginning to slip, his exhausted muscles were becoming limp, and all his strength was ebbing away. He was lost!

A desperate effort saved him.

Pushing one foot against a small outcropping and extending the other horizontally, he leapt, releasing his grip, and threw himself toward a protruding chunk of rock to his left. Using all four limbs, he clung on to it tightly . . .

He remained in that position for a few minutes, overwhelmed by fatigue, trembling at the thought of the immense risk he had just taken. Simultaneously, a bitter wave of regret surged through him like bile. He reproached himself for not having gone along with his comrades' plan, and the realization that his absence from the workshop prior to their departure could hinder or even jeopardize their journey deepened his guilt. His own ordeal was far from over, and he knew it would entail many more challenges. For a moment, the thought of turning back weighed so heavily on him that he contemplated returning to the plantation; however, the memory of the master's abuses rekindled his resolve. He stood, surveyed his surroundings, and finally, spotting a suitable path, he made his way toward a furrow carved by heavy rainfall . . . Before long, he had successfully traversed one of the brow-like ridges of the Salazes.

Of course, he longed for a moment of respite at this juncture, but he had not eaten anything since the night before. His stomach, afflicted not only by hunger but also by weariness and the brisk mountain air, demanded nourishment without delay.

With no provisions at hand, he found himself compelled to scavenge for anything that could alleviate his hunger. His quest commenced with a diligent exploration of the path, as he sought out wild fruit trees that thrived without human cultivation, even in the most inauspicious corners of the island.

But alas, the only fruits he came across were strawberries and raspberries. Far from satiating him, they merely whetted his appetite. Tormented and weakened by the pangs of hunger, he began to fear that he would be unable to continue his journey, that he would succumb to exhaustion in this desolate place. Suddenly, after an arduous climb to the top of a small promontory, he found himself in a lowland where a multitude of the fruit-bearing trees he had been so anxious to find came into view. Date palms, guava, banana, and tamarind-of-the-Indies trees appeared in front of him, profuse with fruit.

At that moment, his boundless joy matched his eagerness to eat the fruits.

But no sooner had he devoured some of them in a famished frenzy than he heard loud barking erupt from somewhere nearby. "The White squadrons!" he thought in terror. He rushed out of the wild orchard and began running in the opposite direction . . .

IV

The Cave—Marie and Frême

OUR POOR MAROON WAS ALIVE. The sky had spared his life, turning his fall into his very salvation.

From the spot where he had fallen, the mountain looked terrifying: with its summit reaching an elevation of more than two thousand meters, it formed a sheer overhanging precipice, holding nothing from head to foot but sparse, detached, inaccessible crags. The maroon hunters gathered that the Câpre, their human prey, was as good as dead down below! However, as he was falling, he had, in an instinctive, abrupt movement, thrust his hands against the mountain-side. Through a twist of fate, he had been able to grasp on to one of those long, thick creepers that sometimes dangle like the ropes along the side of a ship. He let himself slide down, gently, until he reached a sort of plateau nestled amidst the rugged terrain.

He could not believe it; he was saved! All the same, the merciless squad of hunters could still rain deadly rocks down upon him. He immediately looked for somewhere to hide and noticed a sizable opening right at the heart of the mountain, marking the beginning of the plateau. He thrust his head inside. It was a large cave. He entered, unable to see anything at first. But as his eyes grew accustomed to the darkness, he suddenly stopped. What was he seeing? In a corner sat a young White lady cradling a mulatto child at her breast!

Startled by this sudden apparition, he stood frozen in place, his eyes wide with disbelief as he peered into the darkness. The dread of Whites and of ghosts loomed in his mind. He was petrified, and dared neither move forward nor retrace his steps. Meanwhile, the young lady, preoccupied with nursing her child, did not raise her head upon hearing his approach. In a gentle voice, she inquired:

"Is that you, Frême?"

Overwhelmed with agitation, the Câpre stammered out a jumble of unintelligible syllables, incapable of articulating a coherent response.

"Oh, my friend!" she continued. "You took your time

today . . . I heard dogs barking . . . I thought about the squadrons, and I grew anxious for us . . . "

Those last words snapped the Câpre out of his confusion. Understanding that he was neither trapped in a dream nor in the clutches of hunters, he regained his composure and spoke in the calmest tone he could muster:

"Indeed . . . There are dogs and hunters around . . . but the good Lord . . . He is here too . . . " Nervously, he added: "I am not Frême, ma'am . . . "

The young lady shuddered at his confession and raised her head. Her eyes were so full of astonishment that the Câpre tried to reassure her at once:

"Do not fear, ma'am, I am nothing but a wretched maroon, chased here by the barking dogs you heard. I lost my footing and ended up here . . . I have no intention of causing harm to anyone. I am only seeking shelter . . . "

A wave of relief washed over the young lady. She wiped her forehead and sheepishly said:

"Oh! You gave me a fright!"

At the same time, a tall, young Negro strode into the cave. His features were aggressive, his limbs knotted, his body lean and supple.

"What happened? Who frightened you, Marie?" he asked, rushing to her side without noticing the Câpre standing nearby.

"No, it was a misunderstanding, my friend . . . " she continued, visibly relieved at his arrival. Pointing to the Câpre, she said, "'Tis just a poor maroon seeking refuge with us."

The Câpre stammered a few words of apology.

"Oh!" exclaimed the tall Black. He looked at the other in astonishment. "But how in the world did you end up here, brother?"

"Ah, well!" began the Câpre, letting his guard down. "When injustices become unbearable, we've got to abandon ship, you know? The master is a brute. I left his estate and set out for the Salazes, following the path of the maroons. But up on the mountain, I got hungry. Walking around, I spotted a bunch of guavas, but no sooner had I eaten two than the squadrons appeared and let their hounds loose on me . . . I turned to run away—but I couldn't see where I was going. I took a step back and next thing I knew, I was falling—I had been venturing too close to the edge of the cliff without even realizing it . . . Fortunately, I was able to grab on to a vine which led me here."

"Talk about luck!" exclaimed Frême, shaking his head in amazement. "We've been in this cave for over twelve moons, and you're the first, brother, to find your way here. There's no path, neither from above nor below. The only way to get here is by a stroke of chance! But, my friend, you must be tired and famished! Take a seat here on this bench, and let's share a meal together . . . "

He opened his *bretelle*—a kind of knapsack—and took out a few fruits that he had just picked. Marie, who had laid her now sleeping child onto a mat spread out next to her, went and fetched some grilled bananas, sweet potatoes, and a cabbage salad that she had prepared . . . Soon, sitting in a circle in the manner of the Arabs, the two Blacks and the White woman began their modest meal, pursuing their conversation.

"So the masters are still as wicked as ever . . . " observed the young lady, speaking to the Câpre. She seemed sympathetic.

"Always, ma'am . . . If it isn't them, it's those who represent them, and it boils down to the same thing for the poor slaves . . . we suffer the brunt of all this misery and torment. We endure malnourishment and back-breaking labor, yes, but it gets worse . . . you must have heard of the masters, my own included, who scar our bodies with canes, sometimes even cutlasses . . . They shackle us with heavy chains, and we waste away in the stocks or in prison . . . They show no mercy, shatter our bones, sear our faces with firebrands, kick out our teeth, spit on us, and force the filthiest things into our mouths . . . They yank out our hair and even pour boiling water down our throats . . . "

"Stop! Stop! Please!" cried Marie. Her face had paled in horror.

"I understand, ma'am," continued the Câpre, "I understand that this shocks and pains you because you are kind. But why aren't all Whites like you? They believe that we can't feel pain, and if we dare complain to their judges, they turn a blind eye, deaf to our pleas, and label us liars, dismissing us as unworthy subjects. Oh! It's very sad, ma'am . . . and I don't know when the good Lord will put an end to this cursed profession, the Black slave. Even hell is not worthy of such an occupation . . . However, I've heard that many Whites in Europe care about our plight, advocating for our freedom, and that this freedom, which they call emancipation, will be coming soon . . . "

"Oh joy!" piped Marie. "All those injustices will finally stop!"

"If you ask me," said Frême, shaking his head, "I don't believe any of this will happen. I've been hearing these rumors for a while now, and they always talk about emancipation coming soon, but it still hasn't. The Whites will be Whites. They only look out for themselves. The Blacks are their property, their slaves. They're in no hurry to set them free. Some may pity the Blacks and what is done to them, but many others think and claim that it's a good thing; that we are happy as we are and good for nothing but being caged, shackled for life. They support each other, the Whites; they are strong, they are rich. They use the same money they gain from slavery to promote and maintain it. And beyond money, they still promote the ideas of color, race, domination, ships. Everything they get from our labor is proof that slavery works: sugar, coffee, cocoa, cotton, pepper, cloves, nutmeg. Go figure! Besides, how far away is Europe? A deep, wide sea separates us from them, and they have all kinds of things besides us to think about. They don't see us, don't know us; they might be thinking all kinds of things about us. I think they'll take care of those close to them and will forget us because we are far away. They'll take care of the woods and the animals. Not us. They'll make laws, like they do here, for the preservation of plants, fisheries, horses, dogs, and birds; but not for our preservation, nothing to improve our lot. Nobody will care about our freedom . . . "

"Oh!" exclaimed the gentle Marie. "Why would you say that, Frême? God is great. He is mighty, and you know how good He has been to us. He saved us. He will also save the Blacks. Keep faith! The Whites have hearts, they have minds, intelligence. The spirit of justice and practical interest will surely enlighten them, and they'll come to realize that slavery is a wretched thing, and it must be abolished; they'll understand that this is the best path forward for everyone."

"Yes, yes! Ma'am is right," said the Câpre firmly. "Those are fitting words, and I wholeheartedly agree. I put my faith in this cause, for it is just, and it must come to pass. In the meantime, I have fled the master's house; I shall bide my time as a maroon. But let's change the subject, let's talk about you, brother . . . Truly, I can't believe it! How did you end up here with such a lovely White lady?"

"Oh! My lady!" said Frême. "It's a long story. If you won't find it boring to hear—"

"No, not at all," the Câpre eagerly assured him, his curiosity getting the better of him.

"Well then!" continued Frême, "I will try. But I will need Marie's help . . . "

"I'll help," said Marie timidly.

And so, the story began. The Câpre listened attentively to Marie and Frême's tale, of which we shall endeavor to give an abridged account, though we cannot fully capture all its intricacies or its innocence.

V

The Little Negro—
A Childhood Infatuation

FRÊME RETAINED only hazy memories of his parents and his homeland. Snatched away from his native Africa as a young child, he bore no trace of the distinctive tattoos on his face or body that might have revealed his region, people, or tribe.

Nevertheless, he could summon fragments of distant, ethereal memories: his father had been a warrior chief, a tuft of shiny feathers adorning his frizzy hair. He also remembered that it was after a nocturnal ambush, and the terrible clash that ensued, that he had been seized by the enemy and taken from his family.

He was first sold to the Portuguese and brought to one of their trading posts along the coast of Mozambique. After a few months, he was resold to foreign dealers who loaded him onto a ship with the other Blacks they had purchased along that same coastline.

However, the trade had lost its protections of old and was no longer supported by state subsidies. On the contrary, France, in agreement with England, had deployed watch ships to patrol the Atlantic and Indian oceans in an effort to eradicate the practice. As fate would have it, the slaver carrying Frême was spotted and chased down by a French corvette. Before long, it was captured and taken to Bourbon Island, where both the ship and its ill-fated captives were confiscated as possessions of the State.

Frême was overjoyed: he could never have asked for a better master.

Those who have visited the colony might have noticed *la Petite-Île*, a quaint little spot on the left bank of the river, at the foot of the hill in Saint-Denis. It lies as far from the capital as the hill of Montmartre does from Paris, and can be seen from the sea. Perched upon an elevation, it thrives amidst a profusion of trees and small, meticulously constructed huts crowned with vetiver and latania leaves. In the middle is a little house—which has since been rebuilt—covered in shingles and painted in variegated colors. Set apart by its elegance, it towers over the others like a colorful little chapel. This is the encampment of the Blacks owned by the state, a secluded hamlet that shelters those rescued from the clutches of slave ships, including Frême. In fairness, these Blacks are afforded proper care: they are well fed and properly clothed. They are neither beaten to death nor overburdened with tasks. In fact, they are treated with a semblance of kindness, taught crafts and employed in works of public utility. This unique treatment grants them a livelier spirit, a keener intellect, and an overall better condition than their fellow slaves.

Frême, who was part of this elite group, was originally known in his own country as Coudjoupa, which means "lion" or "panther." When he was recruited to work in the colonial workshop, however, the Whites found his name strange, prompting the State to rename him Frême. He was six years old at the time. Bolvin, the manager of the Blacks, who resided in the charming little house aforementioned, took him under his wing. He brought him to his house and offered him to his children as a playmate.

The young Negro possessed a delightful personality and a charming sense of humor. A quick and enthusiastic learner, he effortlessly grasped the tasks at hand, completing them to everyone's satisfaction.

Frême, driven more by his innate character than by obligation, took immense pleasure in playful antics and countless amusing endeavors. The manager's children, two small boys and one girl, found Frême hilarious and laughed at his jokes until their bellies ached. He would mimic the rooster, the dog, the cat, sometimes even the elephant and the ox. On all fours, he would crawl around, punctuating his movements with boisterous shouts of *moo! moo!* Predictably, he soon became the children's favorite toy, an indispensable presence in their lives. They simply couldn't get enough of Frême. He was at the center of every game, every tantrum, every celebration. They dreamed about Frême, yearned for him from the moment they woke up. In moments of distress, it was Frême's name that escaped their lips, and he willingly rushed to their side, tending to his young masters' needs. Even during the rare bouts of disagreement that resulted in minor bruises and scratches, Frême remained steadfast in his devotion, harboring immense love for his companions.

They treated him not as a slave but as a friend. They never ate anything without giving him a taste. Even though it was forbidden, he partook in their meals, enjoyed a share of their treats, and also began to take part in their tutoring lessons and hence learned to read and to write, to everyone's utter amazement and displeasure. But once the threshold of literacy was crossed, there was no turning back for Frême . . . From then on, along with entertaining them, he would help the children with their schoolwork. In this activity, as in others, he showed particular favor to the little girl, as she was younger and gentler. He would sharpen her pencils and quills. He would do part of her homework. He doted on her with great care and attention. During playtime in the yard, he would carry her on his back, playfully imitating the gait of an ox. She seemed grateful for all this, and gave him candy and childish caresses more often than the others!

They were growing up, and their bond of friendship, shared playfulness, and mutual affection were growing too. This innocent and tender camaraderie only deepened with each passing day. It became even stronger when, as adolescence dawned, it came time for them to part, and for Frême to assume his position in the colonial workshop. His anguish was so palpable that it seemed they would need to pry him away from the house, much like the two young boys who were sent to France for their secondary education.

Left all alone, the little girl felt the parting even more intensely. Unlike her brothers, she had no school friends to comfort her, distract her, or erase the memories of the past.

In her solitude, she clung to thoughts of Frême—his theatrical ways and sweet gestures. Likewise, Frême couldn't shake the memories of the joy they'd shared during his time at the manager's house. The kindness, the tender embraces, especially with the little girl, had etched themselves deeply within his being. Her enchanting countenance and graceful presence lingered in his mind and heart. Even amid his toils, she haunted his thoughts, her ever-present smile beckoning him.

Oh, how he longed for the opportunity to remain her devoted servant! He would have given anything to continue entertaining her, brightening her days, protecting her, and faithfully following her every step like a loyal dog! He would carry her when the path got treacherous, protect her from false steps, stones, and thorns! Without him, he feared she might grow bored, stumble, or harm herself. He was no longer at her side, unable to play with her, watch over her, and serve her as before.

How could he hope to recover this special kind of slave-hood, the bliss of pampering her, of fulfilling her every wish? Now assigned as a shipwright, he resided in one of the huts of the *Petite-Île*. All was lost—he would never again be able to draw near her, the lovely little White mistress!

His heart was heavy with such thoughts and every night, upon returning to his straw shack after a day's work, he would stare vacantly at the manager's house, tears welling up in his eyes . . .

Despite his emotional turmoil, Frême was making remarkable progress in his work, drawing nothing but praise from the master carpenter for his meticulousness and exemplary conduct.

Diligent, compliant, and attentive, he was also bright, intelligent, and skilled. It was evident he would become a good subject and worker, and indeed, he was already becoming one. His physical strength grew, his body maturing into that of a man. He even had his own cabin.

However, the memories of his early years in the colony and of the little White girl continued to consume his thoughts, haunting him incessantly. Instead of fading over time, these recollections grew more potent, casting an increasingly profound shade of melancholy upon his daily existence.

He couldn't help but dream of the happiness he had lost. With teary eyes, he would gaze longingly at the manager's house, a forbidden sanctuary that held his angel, the object of his adoration.

Often, deep in the night, overwhelmed by the dark whispers that grief summoned forth, he would abandon his shack and stand alone on the plain. There, his unwavering gaze would remain fixated on the house for hours on end, as if he were enraptured in a sacred and divine contemplation.

He found himself captivated by his own thoughts, which materialized into a vision—a deceiving shadow his longing soul treasured. It was the image of the girl he had once known, the one he had protected like a sister in childhood. Since then, he had only caught fleeting glimpses of her from afar. Now, she had blossomed into a strikingly tall and beautiful White woman, causing tremors to course through him at the mere thought of standing before her. He looked like a fanatic who had broken free from the confines of a madhouse, relentlessly pursuing the guiding star of his religious obsession in the middle of the nocturnal savannah.

And when, his senses having grown weary and his soul tired, he caught himself in that trance-like meditation, a nocturnal sleepwalking ecstasy, he would be plunged into an inextricable chaos of sorrowful and distressing thoughts, which only became slightly more bearable with the shedding of many tears.

VI

The White Girl

SEVERAL YEARS FLOWED BY THIS WAY. All was not bleak, for Frême could take some joy in observing that he had not entirely been forgotten. Sometimes, though rarely, the White girl would catch sight of him. And when she did, she never failed to wave at him—a friendly gesture.

But this fleeting affirmation that they had indeed shared a past did nothing but worsen his grief. The power of his unspeakable affection remained firmly rooted in his heart.

He was almost twenty years old. One night, as he was leaving his shack as usual, he thought he could see sparks rising from the place he daydreamed about incessantly! At first he thought it was an illusion caused by his dizziness, a vertigo brought on by the heat in his head. But seeing that the strange phenomenon persisted, accompanied by a reddish glow, he ran toward it, propelled by a violent sense of alarm. Soon enough, he realized with terror that it was the manager's house itself that was on fire! The flames were already as high as one of the windows. Yet, the whole village seemed to be asleep! Nobody had come running to put out the fire! The house itself, with all its points of egress shut, apart from the usually open casement windows at the top, seemed to be sleeping peacefully amidst the raging blaze!

At such a sight, he felt a terrible storm gathering within him. He let go of all of his inhibitions, his defenses, and, without thinking of calling for help, or of the risk he was taking, he began climbing the side of the house to save its inhabitants from the fire, if such a thing were still possible!

With his naturally lean and strong physique, sculpted by his habitual gymnastics, he soon was able to hoist himself into the house through one of the open windows, into the part of the top floor untouched by the flames.

He ran across the floor, yelling in a heart-wrenching voice: "Get out! Get out!"

No one heard his alarmed cries.

No one except for a distraught girl who emerged from one of the rooms and ran over to the staircase!

But the staircase had turned into a gulf of flaming smoke! Frême caught the girl as she fainted . . .

He carried her to a couch and, wasting no time, as the floor beneath his feet was already smoldering, he collected all the sheets he could find, and fashioned a makeshift rope which he attached to the window's hinge.

Then, dressing the unconscious maiden in the clothes she had left next to her bed, he cradled her in his arms and slipped away from the scene of the fire. He made no noise and met no one, like a lion taking away its prey, and fled with his precious cargo toward his shack, where he laid her down . . .

Stretched upon a Malagasy mat on the floor, the girl remained in the throes of a deep swoon, barely breathing, and seemed to emanate nothing but a feeble glimmer of life, teetering on the edge of fading away forever.

In an effort to soothe her and bring her back, he extricated her from the clothes he had wrapped her in, and dampened a piece of cloth to dab at her white, pale, smooth, angelic face, tenderly parting the dark locks of hair that framed it.

He, Frême, the young Negro, treated that White virgin maiden with such a gentlemanly attitude, such respect!

He knelt beside her, motionless and barely daring to breathe, observing her every slight movement and breath.

He was like a black statue, admiring her, contemplating her with an expression of joy, tenderness, and indescribable concern!

Was he not now in front of the object of his dreams? This adorable, pure thing that constantly haunted his mind, the longing of his childhood and of his manhood alike? He would not have budged from that spot, would not have left this being for his life. Her life, now saved by him, was worth a thousand times more than his own, all the more precious knowing he had wrested her away from death!

As the village bells rang out, rousing the residents from slumber, they cried out and rushed toward the fire. A passerby knocked on Frême's door to alert him, but he did not answer. The house was beyond saving. It was now a gigantic blaze, and all believed that the manager and his family had died, forever lost to the flames.

Then, suddenly, the girl's long eyelashes fluttered—like the petals of a wilted flower blooming anew in a bed of dewdrops. Her eyelids opened partway, revealing her clear and striking sapphire-blue eyes.

Frême, swept away by a rush of emotions, was unable to contain his joy. But at the same time, he started to grasp the potentially dire consequences of his actions. Seeing him crouching there in such a strange position, the White girl thought she was dreaming. She rubbed her eyes, which widened, and whispered in a meek, plaintive voice, "Dear Lord! Where am I?" Her anxious gaze darted around.

Frême, spellbound, found himself unable to respond. With great effort, he managed to stammer a few words about the event in an attempt to soothe her anxiety . . .

Her eyes locked onto him, and she abruptly tried to sit up, but lacking the strength, she slumped back onto the mat, her body curling up like a touch-me-not leaf. She burst into tears.

A few years later, we find ourselves inside a small chapel, at a place called *Le Bernica*, in the charming village of Saint-Paul. An old, venerable White man, clad in humble, austere clerical attire, raises his hands in a solemn gesture to bless a young couple. His lips murmur a prayer, uniting the names of Marie and Frême!

Yes! It was because Frême's nobility transcended his Blackness and the circumstance of his birth; it emanated from the depths of his soul. The one whom he had served when she had been just a child, and saved when she was a young woman, had become poor and orphaned following the fire. She had found in him a generous source of support. And Frême, by the care, attention, respect, tenderness, and absolute devotion he accorded to her, had proved himself worthy of her hand, no matter how White and high-born she was.

Marie herself was immune to any form of absurd prejudice, and guided only by nature and her heart, far from being put off by his color, she found herself attracted to Frême. Her attraction went beyond mere gratitude; it was an expression of everything pure and affectionate that a free and uncorrupted woman might feel for the man she chooses.

Besides, she had lived and grown up alongside Frême; he had been like a brother to her. His black, yet gentle and handsome face was intimately familiar. She couldn't comprehend the mockeries of the other Whites. And if she were to entertain any notion of a color-based hierarchy, she would favor the color of her beloved husband, for beneath the ebony hue of his skin, she had witnessed nothing but worthy qualities and love. After all, despite all our apprehension and disbelief, does there not exist a certain force, natural or perhaps supernatural, a certain fatality, or divine magic, as it were, that brings unsuspecting individuals, often polar opposites, to search for, find, and even attract and love each other? Subjected to the irresistible power of some attractive force, driven into each other's arms through mutual, burning sympathies, they are made to be united.

Frême and Marie had wanted their union to be as holy in the eyes of humankind as in the eyes of the Creator. Despite the odds, they had been able to find, in this country of slaves, one of those noble and true ministers of the Lord who consecrated their union. He was one of those men who invariably preached unity, fraternity, and mercy, regardless of the risks. He was one of those ministers to whom prejudice and distinctions of race and caste are fantastical categories: to them, all men are children of the God they serve.

VII

Racial Prejudice—The Flight

MARIE AND FRÊME were compelled to leave the capital, and had settled in a small, modest house in Saint-Paul. Though the house might have appeared shabby, its location was truly extraordinary: it was nestled beside a captivating pond that stretched the entire length of the village. The view was enchanting, and the surrounding land, in addition to its picturesque beauty, boasted fertile, abundant soil.

Expansive rice fields teeming with quail stretched out in the form of broad, verdant, grassy bands lined with bulrushes swaying gracefully in the crystal-clear waters. In this idyllic setting, grapevines from various corners of the world were entwined upon trellises while an assortment of fruit trees testified to the bountiful generosity of the climate. Here and there huge coconut palms waved their verdant tops in the sky, reigning over the tableau like towering parasols erected to protect from the daytime's excessive heat.

Amid this charming landscape, in addition to her household chores, Marie enjoyed tending to a small garden of flowers and vegetables and raising waterfowl. During the day, her geese, ducks, and moorhens went to frolic in the pond and at night they made their way back home.

As for Frême, he busied himself outdoors. He was given the opportunity of assisting the Baptiste brothers, two excellent shipwrights who lived by the sea, with the construction of a ship. After work, he would head back home and help Marie out with her delicate household duties. Their love and joy seemed to bless the sky itself. How fortunate they would have been if they could have remained forever concealed from the rest of the world!

But Frême and Marie's union could not remain a secret for long. Soon enough, rumors spread across the land that a Negro, who also happened to be a slave, had wed a White girl.

The title of slave that had been ascribed to Frême was false, for he had been part of the colonial workshop and was therefore not a slave. At least, not according to the laws and decrees that had sought to curtail the slave trade.

Yet, as heated minds succumbed to the poisoned legacy of the colonies, the dark specter of racial and caste prejudice reared its ugly head, fanning the flames of anger and indignation. The tempest began.

Since his childhood, Frême had been accustomed to enduring the ignorance, arrogance, and hurtful ways of those privileged foreigners from across the sea. Therefore, he paid no heed to the backbiting and distorted gossip about his marriage that occasionally buzzed into his ears. He refused to dignify them with any response and kept the hurtful words to himself, shielding Marie from their poison.

Unfortunately, however, the gossip, remarks, and vicious insults were only the beginning.

They escalated to physical attacks, with assailants confronting Frême on the road. When he realized that he had the prowess and strength to lay out his aggressors in an instant, thoughts of revenge started to creep into his mind. His frustration grew.

They would gather in bands, lurking around corners. Then, without warning, they would pounce on him, hurling curses and projectiles. They also vandalized his modest house, around which they assembled every night, shouting, hollering, smashing things and making an awful ruckus. "Kill them! Burn the sinners alive!" they would howl. And they did try, on several occasions, to light the house on fire. Even the police, far from calling the tormentors to order, seemed to condone their actions. Marie, anxious all the time, could barely sleep. "Oh, my dear friend," she would say, "we cannot stay in this place. Your life is in peril, and mine as well! Let's leave, swiftly, and seek refuge in the woods. We'll find peace there!" Frême hesitated, concerned about Marie's well-being. But the situation had escalated to a point where he couldn't even leave the house anymore without risking both their lives. Ultimately, the attacks became so vile that they decided that the time had come for them to go live elsewhere, far from the presence and prejudice of the Whites. One night, they mournfully departed their small home by the pond. Frême carried Marie as though she were a child and, together, they climbed to the mountaintop.

They were now marooned and exiled. They wandered from ridge to ridge and glen to glen. Their love and affection for each other became their sole sustenance, enabling them to triumph over the perils, exhaustion, and countless hardships they endured. They struggled to find fruits to eat and thickets to rest in for the night. With little experience in this harsh way of life and lost in unknown territories, their fate seemed bleak. The specter of a somber death loomed before them—slow, agonizing, and potentially worse than any threat they had faced elsewhere. A death devoid of witnesses or succor.

Unbeknownst to them, fate had a surprising twist in store. Like a guardian angel, there was someone nearby, closely following their every step—a kindred soul who, like them, had suffered at the hands of the colonial system and its prejudices . . .

VIII

The Old Negro

THE ONE WHO HAD BEEN silently shadowing Frême and Marie turned out to be an elderly Negro. He had noticed them as soon as they entered the woods. However, being a maroon himself, he had to remain ever-vigilant. The unexpected sight of a White girl and a Black man in that secluded place made him wary at first. He closely observed them, analyzing every move and gesture, trying to decipher their intentions. He needed to ascertain who they were and what brought them to this wilderness. Yet, as he continued to watch, he noticed them exploring, wandering with no sign of hostility. Instead, they seemed like fugitives—hesitant, fearful, and perpetually on edge. His initial suspicion gradually transformed into empathy and compassion for their plight. Suppressing his instinctual mistrust, he decided to approach them.

Frême and Marie were busy in a clearing, gathering legumes to be eaten raw. The elderly man emerged from his concealed position in a nearby bush and approached them calmly.

"What are you doing here, my children?" he asked gently. Caught off guard, the couple of poor pariahs did not answer. They stared at the old Negro, stupefied, unable to utter a word. He continued:

"It is a mistake to eat those plants, my children; they are harmful and could poison you. You must be hungry and weary. I don't have much to offer, but if you come with me, I'll do my best to help you."

Frême and Marie were dumbfounded, exchanging glances in disbelief, trying to comprehend the unexpected turn of events.

"Well! Won't you make an old man happy?" the old man asked with a smile. "Will you not come with me?"

"Oh, come now . . . you, grandfather, are a kind soul!" Frême replied, his voice choked with emotion as he held Marie's hand. "We cannot refuse your offer. We will follow you. We've been wandering without shelter for five days now . . . like maroons."

"How's that, maroons?!" the old man exclaimed in surprise. "Marooned, with a White girl?"

"Sadly, yes," Marie answered, clinging tightly to Frême. "People were furious, they wanted to harm us, all because we dared to marry in the church . . . and we had no choice but to flee for our lives . . . "

"Oh, now you've truly piqued my curiosity! Come, come and share what little I have . . . It's not far; we'll be there shortly." With that, he amiably took hold of Frême's arm, leading the couple on their way.

As they walked, the old man shook his head and continued: "I see . . . I see. Yes, slaves are not the only ones who face harassment in this land, nor are they the only ones who find themselves marooned. I myself, despite this wretched goat hide I wear, lost in this lair of wild beasts, am a free man . . . and this is not to boast, but I have as much right to be respected as anyone else in a town of Whites, because I am a soldier, a French citizen. I have devoted considerable time to serving in the French army, rising through the ranks as a sergeant and commander. I bear the battle scars to prove it . . .

"Well then! After having shed my blood for Europe's freedoms, what do you think happened to me on this island where I was born, and where I thought I would die in peace? They stripped me of my legal protections . . . despite all my papers, all my service, all my freedom, they wanted to make me take off my shoes, make me a slave . . . "

"Make you a slave!" exclaimed Marie in disbelief. "Who dared to do such a thing?"

"An entire family that claimed that I belonged to them because my ancestors did . . . "

"How unjust! And did you not appeal?"

"Appeal to whom, my children? The family had members in influential positions within the administration, they were wealthy and powerful, their influence extended far and wide. When you have such clout, you're never wrong in the eyes of society. So, I chose to remain silent . . . but I never submitted to their injustice, as you might have guessed. I left the town and the White oppressors behind and became a maroon."

"And how long ago was that, grandfather?"

"About fifteen years ago. You must have been very young then, for I reckon the two of you haven't seen more than forty years combined."

"That's correct, indeed!"

"Back then I was fifty. But just like you, in the beginning, I felt weak and ill at ease living this marooned life. Despite my battles in the wilds of Spain, in the Vendée, the bivouacs, the long marches, the counter-marches, and being stranded in the snowlands of Russia after losing my regiment—despite all that I'd been through, those first few weeks here were almost unbearable. I knew nothing of the terrain, didn't know where to find food, or where to hide. When the squadrons pursued me, I would lose my wits, darting through the woods and along the cliffs. I was on edge, bruised all over, and my nerves were frayed. My days and nights were consumed by vigilance. Hunger and thirst gnawed at me relentlessly, reducing me to a mere shadow of myself. I surely would have perished had I not stumbled upon the hole I'm about to show you.

"It was only then that I found some respite, managing to steal a few hours of sleep at night and gather some fruits, storing up provisions for survival. As time passed, I became familiar with the region, adapted to the challenges, and acquired the cunning and experience necessary to thrive. Today, I live comfortably, knowing where to find water, food, and medicine. I can sense hunters and their dogs from afar, while they remain clueless about my hiding place. But here we are, my dear children: as I said, it wasn't very far. Go through this way, but be cautious."

The old man led the two young individuals down a winding path, treacherous and steep, where the mountainous terrain appeared split, cleaved into two distinct sections. They reached the sharp edge of the rock, standing precariously over a deep chasm. On the opposite side, an equally jagged mass of rock loomed before them.

"Where are we going?" asked Marie. She was shivering. "There is no path! We're at the brink of a precipice!"

The elderly man leaned over the abyss, tugged on a rope, and a makeshift bridge emerged, spanning the divide between the two cliffs!

"This is where we're headed!" he said, pointing to the opposite rock, which was shaped like a balcony, an unreachable terrace—the very same rock from which the Câpre, pursued by wild hounds, had miraculously fallen.

"Have no fear, my children. This place will keep you safe." He added: "Hunger, hunters, Whites, or harsh weather— none of it will torment you, I guarantee it . . . And when I call you my children, it's not for nothing: I will protect you, take care of you until the very end, just like a loving father . . . "

Indeed, this old Negro never deserted Marie and Frême after settling them in his cave; his friendship and kindness knew no bounds. He became their devoted slave and divine savior, attending to their every need and ensuring their safety. By day, he darted through the forest and ravines, hunting, foraging, and stockpiling provisions. At night, he slumbered at the entrance of their refuge, a vigilant old watchdog. He regaled them with anecdotes about France, about battles and maroon exploits, sharing his vast experience and wisdom.

Frequently, Frême accompanied him on excursions, training in the art of maroonage. The old man taught him to navigate the woods, scale mountains, outmaneuver hounds and pursuers, wield bow and sling to capture game, and locate freshwater springs, honey, fruits, plants, and roots—anything they might require. Remarkably, the sexagenarian teacher showed astonishing vigor alongside his strong and agile student. His cottony white hair, reminiscent of froth upon the sea, swirled above his dark forehead, yet he exuded a youthful spirit, brimming with strength, health, and vitality.

However, one fateful day during a reckless race, a prickly pear spine lodged in his foot. Despite their pleas, he ignored the injury and refused treatment, disregarding the risk. The dampness of the locale seeped into the wound like poison, and before they knew it, tetanus seized him, taking their beloved guardian away from his adopted children!

Frême and Marie had to pause in their storytelling. They were still very moved by the painful and gripping memory of the good old Negro!

Frême's face had changed, he looked like a man with a stone lodged in his throat: his breath and speech were gone. As for Marie, she gazed at her child through a veil of tears. He had been baptized by the grandfather, who had been the first to hold him . . .

Every morning and every evening, Marie and Frême would solemnly, as if in a church, kneel in front of a black wooden cross outside. It was surrounded by wild flowers and set against a small burial stone, right at the edge of the precipice, facing the Orient.

IX

The Ambush

THE CÂPRE, deeply moved by Marie and Frême's poignant account, found himself engulfed in their profound emotions:

"Oh! You've made me forget everything!" he exclaimed, gently brushing away tears that glistened on his dark cheeks like pearls. "You've made me forget who I was, what I had set out to do, and in addition to your generous hospitality, you have nourished my heart . . . Merry and blessed be you! But alas, our time together draws to a close. I must express my gratitude and take my leave—"

"What? Already?!" cried Frême and Marie in unison.

"Yes, my dear friends, I apologize. I also have a grandfather and, while it's still light out, I would like to go and find him."

"Is he far from here?"

"About two leagues away, near the Piton des Neiges."

"That is quite far still. What is your grandfather's name?"

"Jean," answered the Câpre. "I'm unsure if he goes by any other name."

Marie and Frême shuddered at that name, for their good old man was also named Jean. However, not wanting to worry the Câpre, who barely knew his grandfather, they abstained from telling him that detail, but redoubled their efforts to convince him to stay with them, at least until the morrow. However, the Câpre appeared resolute, his mind made up, and he was eager to continue his journey. Try as they might, it was impossible for them to detain him any further.

The good Marie wished him well, and Frême helped him cross the bridge the old Negro had constructed, offering to accompany him to the other side . . .

Not too far from there, in a deep, wooded ravine, two tanned men, in ragged clothes but armed to the teeth, kept watch. Three or four mastiffs were with them, on the prowl.

"Are you sure you saw them?" one of the men whispered to his companion, both huddled in the brushwood, their eyes fixed on the hollow of the ravine like hawks in search of prey.

"Of course!" retorted the other, "I was perched in the tall palm tree, and from there I had a clear view of the game . . . not that I aimed with my rifle, mind you! They climbed up the hill leading to this slope, and I'm quite certain they'll be coming down soon . . . "

"In that case, we've got them," said the first, "because unless they take the great plunge like this morning's maroon, they have no other way to get down here . . . But hush! I think I heard something! Keep a tight hold on the dogs!"

The Câpre and his host walked into the ambush . . .

"Halt there, or meet your doom!" boomed a dreadful voice, as the dogs and the armed men revealed themselves.

Caught off guard by this surprise attack, the Câpre remained still, too shocked to defend himself. However, Frême, sensing the danger and thinking of Marie, sprang into action, unleashing a ferocious display of strength and courage. Like a lion defending its pride, he confronted the attackers, feeling a surge of power within him.

"Oh! This is your wretched trade," he thundered, his anger blazing. "Nothing but ambushes and cowardice. But I'll have you know, you'll never take me alive!"

No one dared approach him, for he had taken hold of one of the mastiffs, wielding its body around him like a deadly weapon. Swinging the animal with precision, he swiftly knocked out the other dogs!

"He's too strong!" said one of the hunters. "No way to capture him alive!" He aimed his rifle at him, ready to fire at point-blank range.

"Please! Spare him! He'll surrender!"

But before the Câpre could utter another cry, struggling to break free from the grip of the other hunter, a gunshot shattered the air, and the bullet whizzed by. Frême had disappeared . . . He had become one with the hunter. In a single leap, he grabbed his neck.

The murderous assailant, feeling as though he had just been gripped by a snake, dropped his rifle and drew a dagger in its place. But, gasping for air and losing his balance, he collapsed like a lifeless weight. In tandem with the powerful grip of the iron-clad limbs wrapped around him, they tumbled into the mire at the base of the ravine, where they lay still and silent, as immobile as stone.

The Câpre and the other hunter, who were busy grappling with one another, had not been able to take part in this dreadful confrontation, so swift as to be almost unnoticeable. However, on seeing the two bodies fall, they ran over to their comrades, still entangled, and tried to extricate them, to save them . . .

"Oh my God, how terrible!" cried the Câpre. "He's dead!"

Frême's body was gushing blood from a large wound on his left flank. His body lay atop the hunter's, and was all stiff and contracted, but his grip on the hunter's arm—the one with the knife—and on the hunter's throat was just as tight. The hunter's mouth was ajar, his drooping tongue blue and bloody and his bulging eyes bloodshot and lifeless. It was clear that he had been violently strangled to death. They rolled the duo over and over but were unable to take Frême's hands away from where they had settled. Like his opponent, he gave no sign of life.

"Oh! Dear Lord! How terrible! He's dead! And his poor wife!"

"Come, come now, are you done?" retorted the hunter as he shook the Câpre, who had fallen to his knees by Frême's body. "Will you quit whimpering, hideous ape? He killed my comrade, be glad that I haven't killed you for it yet . . . But, if you make me wait, you'll get what's coming to you . . . Huh! You won't even let me cut the paws off this tiger, this disloyal *nègre* . . . Now let's go! Quit your complaining and move! Or maybe I should skin you, that'd be quite the sight, huh? That'd teach you not to complain and run off pretending to be free . . . "

The Câpre had no choice but to comply with the hunter's grim order and leave with him. But as he walked in front of him, he kept repeating in desperation:

"Oh! My God! How dreadful! He's dead! And it's all my fault!"

X

The Capture

AS THEY DEPARTED from the scene, the sun's position in the sky indicated it was five-thirty in the afternoon. The poor maroon was forced onward by his rude and ruthless captor, leaving him no choice but to quicken his pace. They had indeed taken the shortest and easiest route to descend the mountain's slopes. However, crushed by exhaustion and the day's intense emotions, he could barely keep himself upright. Upon reaching the foot of the Salazes, he could no longer bear the strain and collapsed, pleading for a moment of rest. In response, his captor shoved him, crying:

"Move it, you sluggard! You'll rest at your leisure in

your master's hole, but not with me. Where does he live, anyway?"

The Câpre remained silent.

"Hey! Will you answer me? Oh? Playing deaf, are you? Well then! I'll take you straight to the police, and you'll face double the punishment . . ."

This threat, which was against the interest of both the captor—who would receive less payment if he handed him to the police—and his captive—who would indeed endure punishment from *both* the police and his master—jolted the Câpre out of his lethargy, and he responded:

"Sainte-Suzanne."

"His name?"

"Zézé Delinpotant."

"Well, well! You're in for a real treat, my boy! You should be flattered, 'cause I know your master well. And he might be Del-*impotent*, but I can assure you he's no weakling; he's fit as a fiddle!"

"Fit for mischief . . ."

"Really! Is that mischief? Beating up lads like you?"

"I suppose it benefits you . . . it leads to maroons, so you can make a living . . ."

"Ha! Right! You think you're clever? Impressive! You'll see when I thrash you to bits, you *chien de nègre*! Come on, move faster! Quick! And don't resist! Instead of cracking jokes, you filthy toad, brace yourself for the hearty welcome that awaits you!"

Urged on by such a sinister perspective, the Câpre trudged forward like a condemned man marching toward the gallows. His feet, bare and bloodied, could scarcely carry him. With superhuman effort, he persisted, each step an agonizing torment. Finally, after seven grueling hours, the two men reached Sainte-Suzanne, approaching the residence of the aforementioned Zézé Delinpotant around one o'clock in the morning. A broad pathway led to the house, but the master was nowhere to be found. They approached the driver and then the overseer, only to find them fast asleep. The bounty hunter knocked on the door.

"What is it?"

"I caught your rabbit!"

"I see! Hold on . . . "

The overseer, a tall, thin man, soon appeared. His small beady eyes seemed sunken into his pale face, whose hued and pointed cheekbones were framed by long locks of faded, fawn-gray hair. He laid eyes on the Câpre, gripped him by the shoulders and with a contemptuous sneer, he said:

"Oh! It's you, sir! Back from your little stroll, are you? Quite annoying, I imagine. Taking a breather only to end up getting caught and having your wings clipped . . . and don't even get me started on the punishment waiting for you back in your cage!" His voice grew harsh: "Wretched bird! Disgusting rascal! You'll pay dearly for this! You thought you could slip away unnoticed, but not only did you get caught, you also made us waste more money than you're worth . . . " He turned to the captor: "So, how much, for this filthy ape?"

"Fifteen francs, sir! Not too expensive . . . "

"Huh! That's what you think . . . I'm not paying more than two hundred centimes . . . "

"Well, in that case, I'll hand him over to the police," snapped the hunter. "This creature will end up at the municipal pound and work for public utilities. Maybe then you'll realize the daily cost, and that's not even counting the price for his capture. When I asked for fifteen francs, sir, I didn't even reveal the whole story. This rabbit gave me no end of trouble. I caught him in the Salazes, where his companion killed mine and our dogs. If I were to report this information, I could easily have him confiscated from you. The law would be more than willing to relieve you of him . . . "

"Come on, now, here are your fifteen francs! Now get out!" the overseer barked, flinging three five-franc coins at the bounty hunter. Then, pointing a menacing finger at the Câpre, he added: "And you'll be coughing up twice as much for this mess!"

"Kaborda!" he then bellowed to the Black driver, who stood nearby with a long whip. "I am assigning this gentleman to your care. Seems he fancies himself a free man, enjoys the great outdoors. Well, let him savor it before we decide his punishment tomorrow morning. Put his neck in the stocks in the same cell as the wanderers from last night. Let them entertain each other. Understood?"

"Yes, sir!" said the henchman as he seized the poor Câpre and led him to the infernal dungeon.

Yes, that's how it goes in the colonies. The man assigned to mete out punishments does so with a zeal rivaling that of the master himself. In the master's absence, the henchman inflicts terrible suffering on the wretched caste of slaves. He devises new torments, goes on torture sprees, and commits all kinds of abuses, sometimes to the death. The overseer in charge of Zézé Delinpotant's estate was not one of the milder ones—in addition to his own vicious impulses, he knew he had to keep the master content. And the master, to his slaves—as we have seen in the obscene allusion the hunter had made—was a savage beast, known for his legendary barbarity. From the overseer to the lowliest slave driver, the plantation operated under a hierarchy of ruthless tormentors!

"So, you wanted to play the White man, you naughty Black!" taunted the other slave. "What made you run off and waste the master's time like that? No answer? Well, I'll take care of you, just you wait . . . Oh, yes! Let's see if you'll still be pretending to be White after I'm through with you!"

"What do you mean, White?" replied the poor soul, taken aback by the insults hurled at him. "You're just as Black as I am, yet you act as if you're Whiter than the master. All you do is make things worse for us instead of showing any mercy . . . "

"Mercy? To animals like you? I'll give you a taste of mercy with a good thrashing!"

"Well, if you haven't got an ounce of mercy, why don't you just put us out of our misery? Instead, you just drag the suffering out . . . "

"Why? 'Cause it's a good laugh, isn't it? And if we dispatched you, you'd be no more valuable than a dead mule left at the mill . . . We could just swap you out for another one . . . "

"But it would put an end to me, and to the money the master has to spend on me!"

"Well, the master's got deep pockets and couldn't care less!"

"Yes, but we both know that his heart, stone-cold to us, is not indifferent to money . . . "

"All right, shut up now! Here, see what you get . . . "

The driver could not finish his sentence. Arriving at the dungeon, he saw that its door was broken! Wide open!

"Oh, my God!" he cried, bewildered by what he was seeing. "Look at what those demons have done! They smashed, broke everything! What will the overseer and the master say now? They're going to punish me for sure!"

"Stone and iron mean nothing . . . to the heart that desires . . . the mind that ponders," murmured the Câpre.

"What are you saying?" retorted the driver. "I'll show you that there's more stone and iron waiting for you! Let's go, get in there!" he added, pushing him inside the cursed place. "You'll pay for them all!"

Indeed, upon seeing the platform on which he had shackled the three Malagasies completely dismantled, the merciless driver unleashed all his contempt on the poor Câpre. He took him to a corner of the vile cell and bound him by his neck and four limbs, securing him with chains and iron rings affixed to the wall. To add a final touch of cruelty, he left with a fiendish expression and said:

"Now, then, mister free man! You are free to catch some fresh air, if you'd like, and escape like the others . . . "

Alas! To escape like the others! How would he accomplish such a feat? Even if he had wanted to, he would have neither the resolve nor the strength! Overwhelmed with sadness, what could he ask for, except to be left alone? He pleaded with the executioner:

"Leave me be!" His expression was vacant, a reflection of his profound weariness. Despite his galling memories, his current agony, his bloody feet, his throbbing, strained body, and the uncomfortable position he was in—almost vertically propped against the wall—he surrendered to the imperious call of sleep. He crumpled amidst the sea of chains and sank into a deep, profound slumber. His mind soon became engulfed in restless dreams, the kind that follow great torment and overwhelming fatigue . . .

XI

Dreams

THE CÂPRE'S SLUMBER, assailed by yesterday's grievances, soon became a canvas where his darkest, saddest memories proceeded, conjuring dazzling scenes that mingled with feverish nightmares. These scenes, fruits of his troubled mind, presented a series of strange yet lucid images that felt uncannily real.

He found himself back at the *Meeting at the Great Tamarisk*, pleading with his comrades. He begged them not to embark on any rebellious acts or set sail on treacherous waters, but instead to seek refuge in the mountains and become maroons, patiently awaiting the promised liberation.

However, despite his pleas, he witnessed them board a dilapidated boat and depart, trying to return to their homelands in search of happiness, propelled by the spirit of freedom. They bade him farewell but their voices were full of rebuke:

"You're still here? You ignored our counsel, spoke against our plan, and chose to stay with the masters . . . How has that benefited you? You've been hunted, tracked down like a wild goat . . . You have narrowly escaped death, and caused the demise of this brave and welcoming man . . . the demise of Frême . . . "

And each of these words, as they struck his mind, sailed through every fiber of his body, producing within him a kind of general, electrifying tremor. His eyes quivered, his lips trembled, and his muscles twitched as he yearned to see, to speak, to move his limbs, yet found himself incapable of doing so. But when thoughts of Frême surged within his soul, he regained a flicker of control. With a forceful jolt, he wrested himself out of this internal struggle, causing his chains to clatter. He awoke and whispered mournfully:

"Alas! Yes, it is true! I am responsible for his death . . . and perhaps for the deaths of the woman and her child, abandoned in that cave, with nobody to help them! Oh! I'll never forgive myself . . . "

Drenched in sweat, and nervously shaking, he continued to churn these sorrowful thoughts in his mind, in an attempt, perhaps, to temper them, but the more he dwelled on them, the darker they grew, and the weight of guilt for Marie and her child pressed upon him. It was impossible for him to rescue them. His thoughts soon became entangled, and he felt his head drooping as sleep overcame him . . .

Frême then appeared to him, standing atop one of the peaks of the Salazes.

But Frême appeared unnaturally tall, and his chest was covered in numerous gaping wounds.

These wounds resembled deep sea trenches, pouring forth torrents of blood like a whale's blowhole. The crimson streams shot into the air like colossal red rockets, raining upon the entire island.

The terrified inhabitants scattered in fear, seeking refuge in trees, caves, houses, and among rocks. But it was in vain, for none could escape the downpour of blood that crept into every crevice, staining everything red.

And as the blood suffused and submerged the island, Frême began to grow, along with his wounds and the pillars of blood . . . Soon, the entire country became a vast lake of blood, its surface disturbed by a multitude of men thrashing and screaming . . .

Like a rainbow, Frême suddenly vanished.

In his place, a White woman emerged. She was exquisite, divine, and bore a striking resemblance to Marie. She was nursing a baby.

The woman raised the child above her head, like a priest at the altar. Suddenly, everybody who was flailing in the lake of blood turned the color of the child: a fusion of black, white, yellow, and red, akin to the skin tones of certain Orientals and mulattoes.

Simultaneously, a voice resonated from the heavens, uttering words that eluded the Câpre's comprehension, words about transformation, unity amidst diversity, and the destiny of the colonial races.

The woman and the child vanished, much like Frême had. As she disappeared, a solitary droplet of milk descended from her nurturing breast.

This drop of milk fell and spread across the lake of blood, which immediately changed its texture, color, and shape: it became a land teeming with flora and fauna, a rugged terrain with rich and fertile soil. It became a nation where distinctions of color or social status ceased to exist. All of its inhabitants enjoyed freedom, harmony, and the absence of conflict. Rather than enslaving or harming one another, people embraced unity, equality, and mutual support. Love prevailed.

The Câpre had himself changed. He saw himself in this wonderful country. He was one of its peaceful inhabitants.

Yet, alas! While he was enjoying this joyful transformation of his being and the bliss he was experiencing, the driver's voice broke his reverie and plunged him back into his sad reality! He was released from his chains and escorted to the overseer. The terrible hour had come, the time for him to endure what had happened yesterday on the platform and the *quatre-piquets* to the three unfortunate souls whose tale we shall now recount.

XII

The Escape

WE HAVE PREVIOUSLY mentioned the stocks, or *courbari*, in our story, and we must revisit them as we recount the escape of our three Malagasies. The stocks, as a torture instrument, consist of two substantial planks made of dense, heavy wood. These planks are positioned horizontally, one serving as the base and the other hinged on top of it. The planks are secured with iron clamps, and the movable plank can be lifted, lowered, and locked in place using a sturdy peg. This construction resembles an enlarged version of an old-fashioned folding ruler, except with semicircular notches along the intersecting edges that align when the stocks are closed, creating circular openings along its length.

It is within these openings, each measuring no more than six to eight centimeters in diameter, that the prisoners' necks or ankles are secured. Thankfully, after enduring the torment of the *quatre-piquets*, our three fugitives were spared the additional suffering of having their heads locked in the stocks. If that had been the case, their escape would have been impossible, and they would have remained trapped. Instead, they were restrained by their ankles, and in the middle of the night, after spending over fifteen hours in captivity, the Antacime made a daring attempt, albeit with little hope, to take advantage of the slimness and flexibility of his ankles. After some time, he let out a cry:

"Yes! I've managed to free one of my feet from the stocks!"

"Impossible!"

"Yes it's possible! Let me free my other foot, and then I'll come to rescue you!"

"That's wonderful! Yes, please do it, brother!"

"This is harder than I thought . . . it seems one of my feet is bigger than the other, it feels tighter . . . This will take time . . . I'm going to have to dislocate it . . . It's a harsh, difficult chore . . . "

"Come on, brother! You were able to free one, you can do the other!"

"Yes . . . but . . . this wretched foot . . . it's a different breed . . . Ouch! I'm surprised . . . it's so much bigger . . . it's not as flexible . . . and it is stubborn . . . I just hope they don't catch me like this, one leg trapped and the other out!"

"No, brother, I don't think they'll catch you . . . Try a little harder!"

"You mean a lot harder! But I don't care, even if I have to break it, unhinge the bone, it has to come out . . . Oh! Ah! Ouch! Phew!"

"So, did you do it?"

"Yes, I think . . . yes! Free! It's out!"

"It's out!"

"Yes, but it wasn't painless, my ankle hurts . . . I don't care, though. Now it's your turn, brothers . . . "

With these words, the Antacime limped to the padlock at the end of the stocks, which could be slid up and down like certain gates. He forced it until it finally broke and proceeded to free his two companions as he had promised. But they had not fully escaped yet: they now had to get out of the prison, and then the estate—and unmistakable signs indicated that the plantation had not yet gone to sleep. At any moment, someone could stumble upon them, catching them in the act. They anxiously waited until the surrounding noises subsided. Full of resolve, they broke open the doors and swiftly made their way out of the premises. Their escape was a success, and they even took with them some utensils from the cell, including a wooden canteen and some coconut cups, as well as a supply of cassava and sugarcane that they took from the residence. The bounty hunter and his catch did not arrive until an hour later, and by the time the jailbreak was detected, our three Malagasies were already long gone. Nobody knew which path they had taken, nor what they planned on doing.

The next day, word quickly spread throughout Sainte-Suzanne that a small boat, which had been moored to the shore, had vanished overnight. Such an occurrence typically signaled the escape of slaves, their hopes set on reaching the coasts of Madagascar or Africa. However, most often, they would stray with the waves and get lost at sea. The village was thrown into a panic. Longboats were launched into the sea to find the fugitives. An investigation was undertaken, with interrogations aiming to ascertain the nature of the escape and make sure it was not part of some island-wide conspiracy. Nothing was discovered. No one even knew who had taken the boat. The Câpre didn't breathe a word of his comrades' plan and, given that most of the residents had their own share of marooned slaves, it was impossible to determine with any certainty which individuals had escaped.

Eight to ten days passed. Mr. Zézé Delinpotant had made his usual statement to the police. The investigation had died down. A rickety boat ended up colliding and crashing against one of the reefs of *la Pointe des Galets*, at Saint-Paul. The figures who were on board had thrown themselves into the sea, and, buffeted by the waves, they were almost dead when they reached the shore. They seemed to have gone through a great deal of pain and, because they were Black, they were arrested and interrogated. They answered elusively. They were mistaken for slaves who had escaped from Île de France, or Mauritius, and they were handed over to the king's prosecutor. But when they were brought to Saint-Denis, they finally spoke and it became clear that they were, in fact, our three fugitives, who had almost capsized as soon as they had left shore.

The boat they took was not the one that had initially caught the Amboilame's eyes. As they could not find it, they had had no choice but to seize the first unoccupied boat they came across: a rickety, undocked little barque. When they had to cross the breakers gathering and unfurling toward the shore, they got drenched to the bone and their boat filled to the brim with seawater. They were able to empty it and reach the open sea. The weather was calm, so they pushed forward until they lost sight of the land that had enslaved them. Delighted, they began to sing songs of their home country, convinced they would see it again soon. But they had no compass to guide them. They thought they were heading straight to Madagascar, but they were in fact only circling around the colony they were trying to escape. Their supplies would only last them a couple of days, and hunger and thirst soon caught up with them—as did the nasty weather. Weakened, harassed by fatigue and assailed by the squalls, they were forced back to land. When they saw it, they screamed in joy. The wretches thought they had reached their country; little did they know that they were in fact returning to cursed soil.

XIII

The Sentence

UPON LEARNING of the shipwreck and the subsequent arrest of the three Malagasies, a deep sense of unrest swept through the island's inhabitants. Meetings were convened, and the bigwigs among them approached the authorities, demanding swift and severe punishment for the culprits.

"We must," they said, in the warm, entitled tone of the masters, "set a stern example in light of these circumstances. The usual methods of discipline—stocks, cells, *quatre-piquets*, chains, and *fer à branches*—do not sufficiently convey our message. We require something more drastic, something that will crush the spirit of the Blacks and eradicate any inclination to flee the island. Therefore, we propose shattering the bones of each fugitive's four limbs and beheading them! Failure to do so will spell the downfall of the colony, as desertion will proliferate, and with the trade now prohibited, we will face a scarcity of slaves."

Mr. Zézé Delinpotant was the first to suggest this idea as he relinquished his ownership over the accused. The public prosecutor hesitated at first; the punishment proposed was perhaps a little too medieval for his taste. But he was soon accused of negrophilia, and threatened with expulsion from the colony. That left him no choice but to comply, not to the strictures of the law, as they say, but to the sheer inhumanity and barbarity of the masters. The three poor Malagasies were hence judged—what am I saying?—they were brought to a kangaroo court, where the Whites contrived an edict, some law to condemn them *for the crime of having tried to abduct themselves from their master*. The verdict was death, as demanded by the inhabitants.

"Oh!" cried the Sçacalave when the perverse sentence was issued. "Thank you, White gentlemen! You have consumed my tears, my sweat; you have devoured my strength, my courage, and robbed me of my freedom. And now, today, you want to drain me of my blood and kill me. Very well! Thank you! How splendid! At least I won't have to see your accursed—"

He was abruptly interrupted as the police officers gagged and seized him. They dragged him to the prison along with his two companions, the Antacime and the Amboilame. In the meantime, a gallows was erected, right by the sea where the boat had been stolen. The executioner began his preparations, honed his ax. The last time he had used it, he had to strike the accused's neck seven times before finally accomplishing his horrific task. The gruesome beheading required him to literally saw off the head, and he was determined to avoid such an inconvenience this time.

The execution had been planned for the very same day, but because the preparations took longer than expected, it was rescheduled for the next morning. The locals were informed of the change in plans, and were asked to bring a selection of their slaves to the appointed time and place of the ordeal, for them to enjoy the show.

The next day, at sunrise, the executioner, flanked by his assistants and guards, entered the cell where the condemned were still asleep. Waking them up, he said:

"I apologize for disturbing you, my friends, but the time has come—"

"Why apologize?" interjected the Sçacalave. "We should be the ones begging for your mercy, both here and on the scaffold, imploring you to end it swiftly and with as little pain as possible . . ."

"Fear not, my brave children," reassured the executioner, "I have meticulously honed my blade . . . Your courage does you credit . . . I shall carry out this task with the utmost care, and it will be over before you even realize." With these words, he proceeded to tie up the victims, preparing them for the impending slaughter.

Once everything was in order, they were led out of the prison. Dragged through corridors teeming with chained slaves, they were brought under the arch of the prison's grand gate, where a contingent of police officers stood in wait.

"Before we depart from this world forever," one of the three Malagasies said to the warden, who had just completed the final formalities, "we ask for a single favor. You are a good man. You have fed and quenched our thirst like no one ever did before, and you have spared us torment. So please, do us the honor of sharing our farewell and gratitude. Let's share, for the first and last time, a glass of *arrack* together . . . "

The warden, who was a good European military veteran, could not help but accept. He found himself so inspired by their courage and fortitude in the face of doom that he felt tears well up his eyes. His heart softened, and he did more than share a drink with them; he clasped their hands as one would with brothers-in-arms marching toward the firing squad.

The order to depart was finally given, and the prison gates swung open. The sad procession began. The three victims walked with unwavering resolve, surrounded by a retinue of policemen. Trailing behind them, the executioner tightly held a rope, his shoulders burdened by a large gunny sack resembling a bag for game. The handle of his fatal instrument peeked out from the hem.

The gallows stood approximately four leagues away, and a diverse crowd, consisting of people of all genders, social standings, and skin colors, had swiftly gathered along the main road connecting Saint-Denis and Sainte-Suzanne. Some had been forced to come, while others were pushed by curiosity and morbid fascination. Some guffawed as the condemned fugitives proceeded, crying out ruthless jokes about their failed escape attempt and the horrible fate awaiting them. In contrast, a few observed the procession with compassion and pity, their hearts heavy with sorrow. Despite their anguish and internal revulsion, they held their emotions close, refraining from uttering a single word. The three wretched ones were stoic, peaceful, resigned to the fate that was awaiting them. They paid no heed to the stares and jeers of the crowd, exhibiting neither bravado nor weakness. As they neared the site of their imminent doom, they seemed to draw strength from their sacrifice, and the crowd grew larger and more densely packed. Slaves from various corners of the country had been dispatched to bear witness to the spectacle.

It was a scorching midday in June, with intermittent dark clouds intercepting the sun's rays and providing moments of relief from the heat. A humid breeze from the southeast further alleviated the discomfort, allowing the procession to press on without pause. But after three hours of walking, they inevitably yearned for a respite. They came to a halt at a place known as Bel-Air, a picturesque spot. From there, they caught a distant glimpse of the ominous gallows on the opposite side of the river. The platform was shaped like a rectangular table, with a small staircase, ascending from the beach, mounted beside it . . .

XIV

The Execution

AFTER TAKING a brief moment to catch their breath, the victims and their escort resumed their march. Only a quarter of a league remained until they would reach the gallows, and the crowd that surrounded them grew denser with each passing step. The streets were cast in shadow by the throng of restless bodies. Amidst this sea of people, two men stood out. One was a Black of average height, clad only in a loincloth secured around his waist. The other, wearing a similar garment, possessed a more imposing, athletic physique. They had journeyed from the upper part of Sainte-Suzanne and were hurrying along the road, determined to arrive in time.

"Ah!" they exclaimed intermittently, frustration evident in their voices. "We won't make it in time! It will all be over soon—"

As they ran, they ascended every hillock that rose from the ground, striving to catch sight of the main road and the gathering for the grim ceremony.

"Oh! There they are!" one of them suddenly cried out. "I can see the rifles, but we're too late! They've already reached the riverbank. We won't be able to catch up!"

"It doesn't matter!" snapped the other. "Let's keep going! The crowd might slow them down, and we can take the shortcut by the waterfall . . . "

They cut across at a high rock where the river formed a waterfall. Once on the other side, they continued to rush along the water's edge, leaping and bounding forward. Realizing that their elusive target had already crossed the river, placing them at least half a league behind, they increased their pace even more. With determination, they hurried across fields and paddocks, paying no mind to any potential encounters with the masters. Vaulting over ditches and streams as if granted wings, they pushed on undeterred.

"Oh! I think I hear cannon fire!" cried the shorter of the two Negroes in terror.

"Impossible!" replied the other, increasing his pace.

"Listen! Can't you hear the drums? Dear God! Good lord! We're too late! They're dead . . . It's over! . . . "

But the tall Negro was not listening. Like a stag, he launched himself ahead, tapping into the last dregs of his agility and powerful energy. Leaving his friend behind, he swiftly reached the main road. With the fervor of a fanatic, he plowed through the crowd, his voice thundering:

"Come with me, friends! Come! Come! Don't let them murder innocent men! Come, follow me!"

A sudden tremor erupted, rolling from one end of the crowd to the other, as a muffled, growling sound reminiscent of a raging ocean arose and reverberated through the air. The courageous words of the tall Black had struck a chord with the enslaved individuals present in the crowd. In a sudden transformation, those who had been lethargic, silent, and terrified just moments before suddenly grew boisterous and defiant. Emboldened, they followed as one, drawn by the man who had kindled the spark of rebellion.

But hadn't the executions already begun? What else could the somber sound of a cannon and drums resounding in the distance signify?

No matter! The momentum had been launched: they had to act now. People jostled all around the tall Black, pressing against him, while in front of him a path steadily cleared. The roused masses lurched in chaotic heaps, pushing toward the homicidal beach. The line of policemen and gendarmes standing guard was quickly breached: they scattered like butterflies. Even the curious, *shoe-wearing*—that is, *free*—bystanders, seized in sudden terror, had fled in all directions. The crowd rushed to the sacrilegious platform, where innocent blood was already flowing. The heads and limbs of two of the men had already been severed. The executioner was toppled and fell among their still throbbing remains as the last victim was freed from his grasp!

At the same time, the tall Black's companion deployed every ounce of strength he had to pierce through the crowd. As he reached the scene, two cries soared at once:

"It is you, my Sçacalave brother!"

"It is you, my Creole brother!"

The Câpre and the survivor rushed into each other's arms as the crowd, both emboldened by its victory and incensed by the atrocious crime that had taken place, began calling for a revolution and demanding revenge.

But their zeal ebbed as the tall Black, the very one who had awakened their rage, began to speak. That man was none other than Frême, who had been stabbed by the bounty hunter and left for dead in the depths of the woods.

He had miraculously survived his wound, and had been informed of the impending doom of the three Malagasies by the Câpre, who had managed to free himself from Zézé Delinpotant's chains, and had run back to the mountains to rescue Marie and her child. Frême had been unable to resist the urge of his heart, the need to save his brothers, which had empowered him with the heroic resolve he had just demonstrated, even though it meant putting his life at risk once again.

Frême, having quelled the insurrection, extended an invitation to all those who were not directly implicated—which comprised the vast majority—to return to their masters, assuring them of a future deliverance. However, he gathered the remaining group of about a hundred, including the Câpre and the Sçacalave, and led them to the Salazes, settling them along the crest of one of the mounts near his cave. With discipline and determination, he transformed them into an army of resolute and fearless maroons. Dismantling the absurd theory of the Black disposition to servitude, they keep recruiting new members every day. As the masters' abuses escalate, so do their numbers. To this day, Frême remains their valiant leader.

ABOUT THE AUTHORS
AND CONTRIBUTORS

LOUIS TIMAGÈNE HOUAT was a nineteenth-century French writer and physician. Originally from Bourbon Island, now known as La Réunion, he was the author of the first novel in Réunionese literature, *Les Marrons*, which he published in Paris in 1844.

SHENAZ PATEL is a journalist and writer from the island of Mauritius in the Indian Ocean. As a journalist, she has been a Reuter fellow and worked as editor-in-chief of a political newspaper before setting up the arts, culture, and society section of *Week End*, a leading Mauritian weekly newspaper. Patel is the author of four novels, including *Le silence des Chagos* published in France by Editions de l'Olivier-Le Seuil and in English by Restless Books as *The Silence of the Chagos* (2019). She has written numerous short stories in French and Mauritian Creole, as well as five graphic novels, two plays, and translations.

AQIIL GOPEE is a Mauritian writer and poet with degrees in Religion from Amherst College and Harvard, where he also trained in Archaeology. He has published numerous short stories and poems in Mauritius, France, and the U.S., having won the first prize of prestigious Prix du Jeune Écrivain in 2023 for his short story "Insectarium," published by Buchet-Chastel (Paris). He reads classical Arabic, Attic Greek, Akkadian, and Egyptian, and along with a first novel, he is currently working on a literary translation of the Qur'ān.

JEFFREY DITEMAN is a literary scholar and translator working in French, Spanish, and English. He has translated the writing of Pablo Martín Sánchez, Raymond Queneau, and Amalialú Posso Figueroa, and regularly translates journalism and children's literature. His academic research focuses on depictions of cross-cultural influence in narratives of extended kinship from Latin America.

LISA DUCASSE is a spoken word artist, singer, and translator from Mauritius, now living in Paris. She released her first poetry collection, *Midnight Sunburn*, in April 2017 and her first EP, *Louvoie*, in September 2018. She writes in French and English, her two native languages, and her work mostly stems from and builds around the sometimes lived, sometimes imagined life of a traveler and the various homes one finds through encounters, moments, and in places all around the world. She specializes in translation for the screen and the translation of contemporary poetry.